I █████████████████ URN *KE*

... ...en she's 1...
... ...ext book, her favourite
... ...tting her way through a huge
... ...driving her restored 1967 Corvette
roadster—top down, of course.

Connect with Justine at her website, justinedavis.com
at Twitter.com/justine_d_davis
or on Facebook at Facebook.com/justinedaredavis

Also by Justine Davis

Discover more at millsandboon.co.uk

OPERATION HERO'S WATCH

JUSTINE DAVIS

MILLS & BOON

First Published in Great Britain 2019
by Mills & Boon, an imprint of HarperCollins*Publishers*
1 London Bridge Street, London, SE1 9GF

Operation Hero's Watch © 2019 Janice Davis Smith

ISBN: 978-0-263-27414-1

0419

MIX
Paper from
responsible sources
FSC® C007454

This book is produced from independently certified FSC™ paper to ensure responsible forest management.

For more information visit: www.harpercollins.co.uk/green

Printed and bound in Spain
by CPI, Barcelona

ILKA
2009–2017

Chapter 1

You've gotten soft.

Jace Cahill muttered it to himself, since he was alone in his misery. He'd gotten used to the dry and warm—okay, hot—climate of Southern California, and this blustery day in the northwest, driving rain down the back of his neck no matter which way he faced, was getting to him.

Of course, the fact that he'd traveled over a thousand miles by bus, hitchhiking and now walking might have something to do with it. He shifted the backpack that was getting heavier with every step. He was heading in the right direction, and he knew he was in Washington State, on the west side of Puget Sound, but that was about it. As another swirling gust sent a blast of rain into his face, he thought grimly that with his luck, he'd end up marching straight into Canada.

At least then somebody'd stop you and tell you where the hell you are.

And all this to keep a damned promise he'd made years—hell, a decade—ago. He'd done it without thought.

Or at least without enough thought. Cory Grant had been his friend, and it was a promise he surely would never be called upon to keep.

And yet here he was—

He heard the sound of tires on wet asphalt. He turned, spotted an older, somewhat dinged-looking silver coupe approaching. He threw out his thumb, but without much hope, and kept walking as it passed him.

His head came up then, and he frowned. That was the strangest sound he'd ever heard a car make.

The car stopped. And then it began to back up. Straight, steady, not even a wobble. But as it got to a few feet away he heard that sound again. And he suddenly realized it wasn't the car at all, but the dog inside he was hearing. A dog who was barking like crazy, loud, sharp and insistent.

The car came to a stop in front of him. He could see the dog now, through the back window. Dark fur, alert ears and uncanny eyes that were fixed on him. And the teeth. Yeah, the teeth. Although the tail was wagging slightly. It was a different color than his head and shoulders, a sort of reddish brown. But it definitely was wagging. That was good, wasn't it? His spirits rose at the thought of getting out of the storm as much as giving his weary legs a rest.

The driver's door opened, and the barking was instantly louder. A man got out, turned and looked at him over the top of the vehicle. He was tall, lean and looked solidly muscled, but it was the eyes that were the most intimidating. Those were a pair of eyes that had seen too much, and too much of it bad.

"You want a ride, get in," the man said over the dog's continuing vocalizing.

Jace hesitated. But then the dog upped the pitch a notch, and suddenly the man looked like nothing more than a harassed dog owner.

"Please," he said with a roll of his eyes as water streamed down his face. "Get in so he'll shut up."

Jace wasn't sure why the guy thought him getting in would quiet the animal, but the heartfelt plea changed the whole tenor of the thing, and his wariness faded. He reached for the passenger door handle.

The moment he pulled it open the dog went quiet.

"Thank God," the driver muttered and got back in, more than a little wet himself now. When Jace closed his door, the sound of the rain was instantly muted, and with the cessation of the wind blowing it into every conceivable place Jace let out a sigh of relief.

"Thanks," he said.

"Thank you," the man said drily, glancing toward the dog, who now had his head poked in between the front seats. "Happy now, mutt?"

The dog gave a wag of that plumed tail. He had on a collar, Jace noticed, with a blue tag shaped like a boat. The name Cutter was stamped on it, which made him wonder if he was named after the kind of boat. This guy didn't look like an active service member, but he looked too young to be retired. Then again, those eyes...

"He do that often?" Jace asked. "Go ballistic on passing hitchhikers?"

"First time I know of. Buckle up."

Jace did so. Then he twisted in the seat to really look

at the dog. Who was staring at him. Not just looking, staring. The animal let out a low whine. He sounded, Jace thought, almost worried. And then the dog looked at the driver. Gave a short, sharp little bark. The man's head snapped around to meet the dog's gaze. Then he glanced at Jace, then shifted back to the dog. The dog had never looked away.

The man groaned audibly. "Really, dog?"

The dog moved then. Reached out with one leg to paw at Jace's arm. But he kept looking at the man Jace presumed was his owner. If one ever really owned an animal like this.

"Great," the man muttered. "You do realize I'm the only one around right now, right?"

Jace wondered what he was supposed to say to that, but then realized the man had been talking once more to the dog. The dog, who let out an odd little whuff of sound that sounded crazily like, "So?"

The man sighed. Pulled the car over to the side of the road, which made Jace even warier; given the lack of traffic, they could have sat there for an hour before another car came by.

Then he turned in the driver's seat to hold out a hand to Jace. "Rafe Crawford. And this pain in the...neck is Cutter."

"I gathered," Jace said, shaking the offered hand, noting the strength that was obvious but not expressed with any declarative squeeze. This guy had nothing to prove. "The tag."

"Yeah."

He waited, and belatedly Jace realized what for. "Uh… Jace Cahill."

The man named Rafe nodded. "So," he said, sounding like a man resigned to an inevitability he wasn't looking forward to, "are you heading to or from?"

"To or from…what?"

"Whatever your problem is."

The first thing Cassidy Grant saw when she opened the door was the dog. He was a pretty thing, thick black fur over his head and shoulders changing to a reddish brown over his back and hindquarters. Thick, warm and rich looking. But she barely noticed that, for the animal was staring at her intently with dark, amber-flecked eyes. Not malevolently, just…staring. Sitting very politely, but staring.

"Hi, Cassie."

The quiet words, in a low, rough-edged voice, snapped her gaze upward to the man who had stepped up to stand beside the dog. Her breath caught. Only then did she see how thoroughly she had convinced herself he wouldn't show. And he didn't look like the boy from down the street she remembered; his hair was just as dark but longer, his clothes a little ragged and his face unshaven. He was carrying a backpack that looked a bit worse for wear, as was the heavy jacket.

But she couldn't mistake those vivid blue eyes, or that jaw, or that mouth. And even if she could, there was the little scar below his left eye. The scar she had given him the day he'd caught her jumping off the roof when she was eight. Nearly twenty years ago now.

"Jace."

"Sorry it took me so long."

She tried to shake off her shock. He seemed to notice—but then, hadn't he always?—and frowned. "I…didn't expect you at all."

The frown deepened. "But you called."

"You didn't answer."

"I…gave that phone to my mom. She played me your message."

His mom? Cassidy remembered the tiny, sweet woman from when they had lived down the street. Before they'd broken her foolish heart by moving away.

"How is your mom?" she asked, feeling suddenly derailed by the niceties of civility.

"Fine, now," he said, and there was satisfaction in his tone.

Now? She hadn't been? She was about to ask when the dog nudged her. "You brought your dog? He's beautiful."

"He's not mine. He just… I'll explain that later." Then, like the Jace she remembered, he cut to the heart of it. "What's wrong? You…weren't real clear on the voice mail. And when I tried to call back—"

"I… My phone died." Which was true. What she didn't say—yet—was that she'd let it die, after turning off any locating function she could think of, because her mind was full of ideas about how the GPS and other things she didn't even know about would lead right to her. Silly, but…

"What is it? Your message… You sounded scared."

"I was."

She saw him take in a deep breath before he asked for a third time, although softly now, "What's wrong, Cassie?"

That did it. He was the only one she'd ever allowed the nickname. She'd liked when he'd used it, because it was something only between the two of them. Even her family didn't use it. It was Jace's alone, and that had made it, in her teenage brain, something…intimate. But now it smashed through her walls, and for a moment the fear surfaced.

Jace reacted instantly. He reached out to steady her. As he always had. Even the dog noticed; she heard the soft whine. And the animal was pressing against her knees. Between them she felt oddly steadied, as if an earthquake had stopped.

"I brought help," Jace said.

"Is he a guard dog?"

"Do you need one?" His voice was suddenly sharper.

"I…feel like it."

"Then you've got one. Three, actually."

"Three?"

He looked behind him. And for the first time she realized the dog wasn't his only company. A man came out of the trees on the north side of the house. A stranger. Tall, lean, dark haired and intimidating in a way she couldn't quite put words to. He was walking past the older silver coupe parked in the driveway behind her own SUV. Walking with a very slight limp Cassidy didn't think she'd even have noticed had she not been at the perfect angle.

"Jace, I don't—"

"He works for a place that specializes in helping people with trouble. At least let's talk, all right?"

It was ridiculous. True, she'd called on an impulse she'd regretted, but she had called him. And to her amazement, here he was. So now she was resisting even letting him in the door?

The dog whined again, and she looked down at him. Those dark, gold-flecked eyes were fastened on her. He nudged her, as if asking for attention. Automatically she reached down to pet him. The feel of the silky dark fur on his head was oddly soothing. He kept looking at her, as if trying to tell her it would be all right.

She nearly laughed at herself, putting human thoughts in a dog's head. She'd known some clever dogs who had a knack for reading human emotion, but that was a bit much. Still, it steadied her to the point where she realized that she was leaving the person she'd called for help literally standing out in the cold.

"I'm sorry," she said as the other man reached the porch, "come in. I'll put coffee on—it's cold out there."

The moment they stepped inside and she got a closer look at the man who had been driving the car, she almost wished she hadn't. Those eyes weren't just intimidating, she guessed they could be terrifying.

"No one around," the man said, "except a guy next house over, chasing a cat."

"Mr. Snider," Cassidy said, then processed the rest of what he'd said. That while she and Jace were talking, he'd been…what? Checking out the neighbors?

He works for a place that specializes in helping people with trouble.

She would not, she decided immediately, want to go up against this man. And the idea of having him on her side was admittedly heartening. But it was silly to think, for if he was a pro, then he was going to think just like the police—that either she was imagining things or the threat wasn't real. Not that they'd said that, they'd been very polite, even gentle, but in truth she had nothing to give them in the way of proof.

She gestured them, including the dog, who seemed to understand, into the living room, then walked toward the kitchen. She wanted to run, but they could still see her and she didn't want it to be quite that obvious that she was nervous, still wishing she'd never made that call. It was only that she'd decided Jace wouldn't show up and then he had, she told herself. It was the unexpectedness of it.

When she came back with coffee, she was still edgy, but better. She took a seat on the couch, safely at the other end from Jace. The man Jace had introduced as Rafe sat in one of the armchairs, the dog sitting politely but alertly at his feet.

"He's very well behaved," she said, aware even as she said it that she was avoiding the reason for them being here.

"He's got good company manners," the man said. "You should have seen him at his owner's—my boss— wedding, in his bow tie."

She laughed, and suddenly the tension eased. She saw a glint in the man's eyes that told her that had been the purpose. Perhaps he really did specialize in helping people, for despite his intimidating looks, he'd eased her strain.

"Cassie?" She looked back at Jace when he spoke, again using that name she'd only ever allowed him. "You really are scared. What's wrong?"

She took a deep breath. If he'd actually come in response to her panicked call, she had to at least explain, didn't she?

Begin with what she thought they should know first.

"The police don't think anything's wrong. Because I have no proof."

"Proof of…?" Rafe then, prompting when she didn't go on.

Finally, she said it in a rush. "I have a stalker."

Chapter 2

Once Cassie had started, the words seemed to rush out of her. "I know, who'd stalk me, I'm not the type."

Jace had had a moment to really look at her now, and he thought she was very wrong about that; his best friend's younger sister had grown up quite nicely in the years since he'd last seen her. She'd been sixteen to his eighteen then. The eyes that had been a sort of vague color then were an amazing mix of green and gold and darker flecks, a combination that he supposed would be called hazel. Her hair was the same medium brown, but with lighter streaks that spoke of days in the sun even here, where it was usually only a summer visitor. Her nose still had that slight upward tilt, but her mouth was fuller. So were the curves—

Damn.

Cory's laughing words, spoken more than once, came back to him. *She's the brain of the family—I got the looks.*

That might have been true then; quiet little Cassidy Grant had been a bookish girl who likely would have faded completely into the background for him had it not been for one thing; she had ever and always been able to make him laugh. That brain Cory had always joked about was indeed present, and part of it was a knack for retorts to her brother's teasing that left Jace roaring both at what she'd said and the look on Cory's face.

She's the brain of the family—I got the looks.

And if the world ever finds a useful purpose for long eyelashes and dimples, they'll beat a path to your door.

Poor Cory never could figure out if she was complimenting or insulting him. Jace had just grinned at her and said he hoped she never got that mad at him.

I wouldn't. I couldn't.

It came back to him, the way she'd looked at him so earnestly. And how Cory had later rolled his eyes and said, "Are you really that dense? She's crushing on you."

He shook off the memories. "Looked in a mirror lately?" he asked her.

Cassie blinked. Drew back slightly. Slowly, she smiled. "That was very nicely done. Thank you."

"Wasn't nice. Just true. But that aside," he said with a glance at Rafe, "do looks really have much to do with the way a stalker's brain works, who he fixates on?"

"Not always," Rafe said. "It might start that way, looks or fame, but often it's something else that sends them down that path. Almost always driven by the delusion that there's a connection between him or her and the victim. A personal one. And that if they only knew it, they of course would want to be together. Or they do know it but are being forced to deny it by other, outside forces."

Cassie looked at the man curiously. "Were you a cop before you worked for…whoever you work for?"

"No. Just learned a lot along the way with Foxworth."

"Foxworth?"

Jace grimaced. "I'll leave that one to you," he said to the other man. "But I'd suggest leaving the dog out of it. She's pretty empirically minded."

Rafe glanced at Cutter, then back at Cassie. "So am I. Accepting Cutter is…what he is was a tough go. But I also know he's never been wrong."

"Wrong?"

"When he brings someone to us."

Cassie gave Jace a sideways look. With a sigh, he told her the story of their rainy encounter. But when it came to explaining Foxworth, he left it to the man who was taking it all with an utterly straight face. And he left out the part where he knew darned well Rafe had checked him out before they'd headed back out into the rain; that phone call he'd made was too pointedly out of his earshot. He pretty much knew what the guy would find, so he didn't worry about it.

"So," Cassie said slowly when they'd finished, "you work for this Foxworth Foundation, helping people in the right turn lost causes into wins, for nothing, and then your boss marries the woman who owns this dog, and you discover he's got a nose for finding those people? Is that about it?"

Rafe grinned at that, and it changed his entire countenance. "Best summation I've heard. I'll have to remember it, because I'm not the best at explaining it."

Cassie looked inordinately pleased, and Jace was irritated that that irritated him.

Irritated squared, which makes it even bigger than irritated twice over.

Cassie's long-ago explanation, which had been about her being angry at both her brother and him over… something, echoed in his head.

"And," Rafe added, "everybody else is off for the holiday, so you're stuck with me." Jace saw him reach down and scratch behind the dog's right ear. "And this guy, who's worth about three of any of us."

"Who decides who's in the right?" Cassie asked, and Jace's gaze shot back to her; he had asked exactly that himself. Rafe gave her the same answer.

"That's the best part. We do. Nobody decides for us."

"About this stalker," Jace said, dragging them back to the subject. "You said you didn't have a description."

"No," she said, "but I swear, someone's been following me."

She looked at Rafe, as if doubtful he'd believe her. As if he'd read her thought, he said quietly, "And watching you?"

Her breath caught audibly. "Yes. How did you know?"

"Saw some sign under the trees out there."

Jace's jaw clenched as Cassie paled. "He's been hiding in my trees?"

"Someone's been in there. Enough to leave a sign. What can you tell me about him? It is a him?"

"Yes. I don't know who, have no idea why, or even what he looks like, but…"

"Is that because he hasn't gotten close enough, or because he's masking himself somehow?" Rafe asked.

"Both," she said. "I mean, he does stay back, but he wears hoodies with the hood up, or knit hats with a scarf wrapped around his neck and face like it was thirty below. Oh, and gloves. The thin, stretchy kind."

"Interesting," Rafe observed. "A bit overkill."

"Maybe he's not from here," Jace said. "I grew up here, never thought forties were cold, but people in California would be dragging out ski wear."

Rafe nodded. "Could be."

Cassie looked at Jace. "You were in California?"

He nodded. "That's what took me so long. I—"

He stopped abruptly. He had just noticed the photograph on the shelf behind her. A family photograph, taken on a sunny summer day on the beach at the lighthouse a few miles away. He remembered going with them that day, vividly. And he remembered this picture. Mrs. Grant had asked someone walking by to take it, and Jace had edged out of the way.

And where do you think you're going, Jace? Get over here!

He remembered gaping at Cassie's mother in disbelief. And then her father had come over and grabbed his arm to pull him into the shot. He stared at it now, saw the two loving parents, Cory next to his mother, Cassie next to her father, and…him. In between both adults, with both their arms around his shoulders. As if he were theirs. As if he, of the three kids, was the one who needed them most.

He found himself blinking rapidly. Because that had been nothing less than the truth.

That's what took me so long.

Cassie felt a twinge of guilt at her earlier assumptions, that he wasn't coming at all. She should have known. This was Jace, after all. Not her brother, who didn't quite seem to understand what a promise was. Like his promise that this or that batch of trouble was the last one, when in fact he'd skated on the edge of trouble most of his life. Not her brother, who couldn't even be bothered to return her phone calls.

Call Jace. He'll come. He promised.

Cory had said it with a shrug, as if the world knew that Jace's word was golden. And apparently, it still was. Because he'd simply come when she'd made that near-panicked phone call the night she'd seen that shadow lurking outside her bedroom window.

And then she noticed Jace was staring past her. The lighthouse photo? Was that what was making him look so...so...

Thankfully, Rafe brought them back to the matter at hand.

"The police didn't think that was enough description?"

She grimaced as she refocused. "More that it could match any one of a dozen people on the street at any given time. Tourists come through here on their way to the national park, and a lot of them are bundled up, like Jace said."

"But you're sure he's following you?" Rafe asked.

Maybe it really was all in her head. Why on earth

would anyone fixate on her, after all? She wasn't famous, she certainly wasn't rich; the shop was barely getting by. And she wasn't drop-dead gorgeous; she hadn't broken up with anyone recently—hadn't dated anyone in a sadly long time—nor had she had any angry encounters with anyone, male or female. No new people or angry customers at work, where she generally kept to her office in back of the florist shop except when she had to cover the counter or made deliveries to help out. No passing contacts with people while shopping or picking up her morning coffee. The answer to every question the police had asked was no, including if she had any idea why someone might be following her.

"I know it sounds crazy, there's no reason for anyone—"

"Sometimes all it takes is an attractive woman alone," Jace said. Cassidy's head snapped around. She stared at him. "What?" he asked, looking utterly blank.

She reined in her pulse, laughing at herself for the silly jump it had taken. *That's all it takes, Jace saying you're attractive? Didn't you outgrow that long ago?*

Not, she thought, that any woman's pulse wouldn't jump. He was still Jace, after all. Sexy cute, with those bright blue eyes and that kind of wild dark hair that always looked a bit windblown.

Do you even own a comb?

That's what fingers are for.

She nearly blushed at the years-old memory. He'd answered her question with a glint in his eye she'd been too young at the time to understand, and it wasn't until much later that she'd realized he hadn't necessarily been talking about his own fingers. She'd finally gotten it the day she'd seen him outside the gym, with Kim Clark running her fingers through that thick hair. The rather predatory social leader, the kind who sniffed audibly at studious types like herself, had set her sights on Jace the day after he'd won his first judo competition.

To his credit, Jace hadn't fallen for it.

She's a user, Cassie. She never even glanced at me before. Besides, she doesn't get me.

But she did. Where most people found his quirky way of seeing things puzzling, she found it fascinating. She always had.

She found him fascinating. She always had.

"Cassie?"

She realized she was still staring at him. "Sorry. Memory bomb went off."

He looked startled, and then he was grinning. That devastating, flashing grin that didn't just light up his face, but the whole room he was in.

"I can't believe you remember that."

I remember everything about you. But "It's still the best description ever" was all she said. Then she shifted her gaze—reluctantly—to Rafe. He was watching them rather assessingly.

"Sorry, I don't mean to be rude," she said quickly.

"You have history," he said simply.

Oh, yes. And I just got smacked with the fact that for me, it's not history at all.

Chapter 3

"How long has this been going on?" Rafe asked her.

Jace felt oddly relieved that he was bringing the conversation back to the matter at hand. He wasn't sure why—he'd known there would be memories involved, simply because Rafe had been right, they had history.

"Almost three weeks," Cassie answered, then quickly amended, "That I'm aware of. It could be longer. I might not have noticed right away."

"Where?" Rafe asked. "Work, home?"

"Both. At least, I think it's the same guy. I haven't really seen him here, only his shadow. At night."

Jace frowned. "His shadow?"

"He—assuming it was him—was outside my bedroom window."

Jace swore under his breath.

"That's…when I called you. I got scared that night."

"I would think so."

"Where did you first notice the guy?" Rafe asked.

"Outside the shop. He was just hanging around. And he looked…"

"Sketchy? Edgy?" Jace asked.

"More…watchful. Like he was waiting for something. But he wasn't looking at the street or sidewalk, he was looking at the shop."

"And what did you think he was there for?" Rafe asked.

"No idea," she said.

"But what did you think?" he asked again, gently.

Cassie looked puzzled. "Usual stuff, I guess. He was waiting for someone—we had a couple of customers inside. Or he wanted to come in and hadn't worked up to it yet." She smiled. "Some guys have an amazingly hard time deciding to buy flowers for someone."

"I buy them for my mom," Jace protested.

Cassie blinked. Looked as if something had clicked in her mind, but she only said, "That wasn't aimed at you."

"Oh. Sorry." He grinned rather crookedly. "Must have been from being around you guys growing up. I never thought flowers were scary."

"I know," she said, and this time her voice was soft, her smile fond. "I remember you used to ask my mother what they all were called. And the lilies were your favorite."

Now he was embarrassed. "Yeah," he said. "I liked how they looked so delicate, but if you didn't take care they'd mark you forever with that orange stuff."

"Attack of the Tiger Lilies."

He had to laugh as she quoted the old title he'd made up as a kid for a horror film starring the tiger lilies simply because he liked the name.

And yet again Rafe had to steer them back to the matter at hand.

"What else did you think or wonder about him that first day?" When she hesitated, Rafe leaned forward, elbows on his knees. "Sometimes your brain processes things faster than your conscious mind is aware of. So you have a thought that seems out of the blue, or baseless, when in fact there was an entire thought process that brought you to it."

"I'm not sure what you mean," Cassidy said.

"He means—I think," Jace added with a glance at Rafe, "like when you see a bluebird. You think you instantly know it's a bluebird, but really it's a process. First you see that something's there, then recognize that it's a bird, then that it's blue, and then that it's not a blue jay, and voilà, you arrive at bluebird. But you're not conscious of all those steps."

She was smiling by the time he was halfway through. And Rafe, thankfully, was nodding, so he'd been right.

"Okay, I get it. But—" she gave Rafe a doubtful glance "—I'm not sure how it applies here."

"When he kept hanging around, did your thoughts about what he might be up to get worse?"

"Oh. Yes," she said with a small laugh. "I started wondering if he was working up the nerve to steal something, or rob us." As if she'd heard her own words, her eyes widened. "Do you think that's what it was? That he was…what, casing our shop? That would be pointless— we really don't have much cash on hand. Most people use credit or debit cards."

"Assuming the shop's cash is what he was after," Rafe said.

"But what else?"

"Did he make you nervous?" Jace asked. "In a... personal way?"

"You mean did I feel like it was me specifically he was watching? Not then. Not until I started feeling watched around here, at home."

"What made you think it was the same man?"

Cassie let out an audible breath. "That's what the police asked. And since I've never really seen him when he's been here, I still don't have an answer other than odds."

Jace knew she meant the odds that in a small town like this there would be two men hanging around the two places she frequented most. He agreed, but he wasn't sure the clearly experienced and likely more suspicious Rafe would. But the man was simply nodding, looking thoughtful.

"Too coincidental," Jace said.

"Yes." Cassie sounded relieved that he understood.

"I need to ask you some questions," Rafe said. "And some of them might seem not pertinent, maybe even impertinent."

Cassie drew back slightly, looking at the man. "Not a word I'd dare to apply to you."

Rafe smiled, just slightly, and Jace had the thought that it wasn't exactly a pleased smile. And Cutter shifted suddenly, from his polite, alert posture to leaning slightly against Rafe's knee. The man's hand went to the dog's head, to scratch behind his right ear, and it had the feel of an automatic gesture, done so often it didn't require thought any longer.

It was almost like the dog had also sensed that smile hadn't been a happy one and had moved to comfort. He remembered how his childhood dog, Max, had always seemed to know when he was sad or upset and had come to comfort him.

And remember what that cost him.

He shoved away the memory as Rafe spoke again.

"I'm sure you've already thought of the obvious," Rafe said, "but I have to ask anyway. And if I ask what seems like the same thing again but in a different way, don't feel hounded. Sometimes just a different way of phrasing can trigger different thoughts and ideas."

Jace listened as the man asked a string of questions. Some he could have answered himself, and he nodded when she did so exactly as he would have expected. Cassie would never get into an argument at work—she was the peacemaker, probably learned from years of trying to broker peace between her brother and their parents. She had a knack for seeing things from another point of view and acknowledging it without ever conceding her own. And she had worked in the flower shop since she was a teenager, so she knew her stuff. Not to mention, knowing her, she worked harder than anybody else.

Unhappy customers? No one that stayed unhappy.

You don't have to agree. Sometimes all people need to know is that you hear them, understand where they're coming from. That was Cassie's philosophy, and always had been. Nobody could stay mad at her for long.

Traffic accidents? No, Cassie was very careful.

Upset neighbors? He nearly laughed at that one. Unless she had very much changed, Cassidy Grant was who you came to if you needed a favor—your dog walked, your cat fed, your kid watched at the last minute; if she could, she'd do it.

True, he hadn't had contact with her in years, but that was who Cassie was at her very core, and he doubted she had changed much.

Boyfriend?

Jace went still. He should have realized that one was coming. Felt silly when he realized he was holding his breath, waiting for her to answer.

"No."

No explanation, just a flat no. He could breathe again. And he'd analyze what the hell that meant later.

"Exes?" Rafe asked.

She glanced at Jace. A quick flick of a look, but he was certain he'd seen it.

"Not…recently."

"How long ago?"

She answered neutrally, "Nearly two years."

Two years? How had a woman like Cassie gone two years without having guys beating down her door?

"Long time," he said, his voice coming out a bit gruff. She only shrugged.

"How were the partings?" Rafe asked. Belatedly, Jace realized this could be exactly what they were here about.

"Agreed upon, if not amicable," she said, her voice still betraying no emotion at all. Odd, he thought, she'd always had trouble hiding her emotions before. He found he wasn't particularly happy that she'd learned.

"How far from amicable?" Rafe continued pressing.

"Not very. And what wasn't was on my part."

There it was, finally, a trace of…something. Pain? Hurt? He felt suddenly guilt that he was glad of it, but he couldn't deny this cool demeanor was bothering him. Cassie had always been quiet, but never cool. Even back then he'd often suspected she was quiet because inside she was very much not cool.

And sometimes those hazel eyes had been dark with emotion, absolutely stormy. Cory had asked him once how he always seemed to know when she was in a mood. "It's right there in her eyes," he'd answered, surprised that it wasn't obvious to everyone.

"I'll need names," Rafe said. At her edgy look he added easily, "Process of elimination."

"Oh."

"Who was the most recent?"

"Steve Larsen. He's a teacher at the middle school."

"How'd it end?"

"He went back to his ex-wife." She gave a half shrug. "I understood. They have two young children. They remarried, and I'm happy for him."

"Who was before that?"

"Tim Sparks."

Jace gaped at her. "You dated the jock?"

Cassie shifted her gaze to his face. "Says the judo champion of the entire school district?"

"Yeah, but Tim, he was…"

"Yes, he was. But he's grown up a lot since he used

to strut around campus. Having your girlfriend die in a car accident will do that to you."

He blinked. An image of the girl, the classic cheerleader type who had been the perfect match for the football captain, formed in his head. They'd been the cliché couple, each a star with their own posse, and together the superstars of their little world. "Carly's…dead?"

She nodded. "Right after their graduation. You'd know that if you ever bothered to keep in touch."

"Been a little busy," he said, stung.

"Hmm."

He lapsed into silence as Rafe continued to ask her questions. He only half listened, because he was trying to picture quiet, clever Cassidy with the outgoing, unserious Tim. But maybe the guy had found her quiet calm soothing after what had happened. When she said he'd gone on to become a successful attorney, he thought maybe that was a clue.

Rafe stopped to make some notes, and Jace blurted out, "Was he driving?"

As usual, Cassie had no trouble following, even though it had been a few minutes since she'd told him.

"No. But it was his car."

"So he felt responsible."

She was looking at him rather intently. "No. That would be something you would do."

He blinked. Her tone had been so neutral he couldn't tell if it had been compliment or accusation. Knowing Cassie, probably both.

Cutter was suddenly on his feet. He was looking

from Cassie to him, then back, his expression oddly puzzled.

Don't try to figure her out, dog. She goes way too deep.

The animal walked over to her, rested his chin on her knee. She looked bemused but pleased and put a hand on the dark head. He watched her face as she looked down at the dog. Saw the slow smile dawn, wondered if she was feeling what he had felt the first time he had stroked Cutter's head in the same way. Wondered what it was about the animal, what knack he had.

Wondered when Cassidy Grant had gone from quietly cute to utterly beautiful. And the thought of her in genuine danger made his stomach knot.

"I have a question," he said abruptly. "About the elephant not in the room."

Her head came up.

"Where the hell is your brother?"

Chapter 4

Cassidy managed not to recoil at the anger in Jace's tone, but it was a close thing. "Hell if I know," she retorted.

Jace looked surprised. That she'd echoed his curse? Or that it was about her brother, whom, for all her teasing, she had adored?

A lot has changed since you were here.

It wasn't that she didn't still love Cory, but... And then, belatedly, something else occurred to her. "Don't you know where he is?"

Jace made a face that matched her sour tone. "I haven't talked to him in..." He trailed off, then finished with a rueful expression after he apparently figured out just how long it had been. "Four years."

She frowned. "But you two were best friends."

"Yeah. Funny how that ended once he knew I couldn't lend him money anymore."

He looked as if he regretted saying it, so she hastened to say, "I get it. I didn't hear much from him after the bank of Cassidy closed up, either."

He frowned. "Are you…in financial trouble? With the shop, and I thought your folks had a little life insurance—"

"Not in trouble, just…tight. The shop's breaking even, but no more. I cut Cory off after he blew through his half of the insurance money in a few months. It wasn't that much, only fifty thousand, but…" She waited for the look, the one some people gave her, accusatory. How could she cut off her own brother if he needed help?

Instead he just said softly, "Good for you." She blinked, surprised. "I know what he likely blew it on," he explained.

She felt a jab of relief that she wouldn't have to explain. "Is that why you stopped loaning him money, too?"

"No. I—" He cut himself off, gave a sharp shake of his head. "Never mind. Irrelevant."

She supposed it wasn't relevant, but she couldn't help wondering what had made him say it like that. With such an edge.

"Are we sure of that?"

The inquiry sounded mild compared to Jace's edge, but Cassidy doubted anything coming from the man who had been sitting so silently yet still was such a presence in the room should be taken lightly.

"What do you mean, Mr. Crawford?"

"Rafe, please. I already feel old enough just getting up in the morning."

He said it so wryly she couldn't help but smile. "All right, then, Rafe," she said. "Are you saying my brother might be connected to this?"

It seemed an impossibility to her, but she kept her tone neutral. She'd learned a lot about self-control when it came to her brother.

"That depends," the man said, shifting his steady gaze to Jace, "on what exactly he was spending that money on."

"Not drugs," Jace said, with a quick glance at Cassidy. "He was never into that, or alcohol. But he was… always looking for the easy way. The big thing that was going to make him really rich."

"There are many people who would consider having fifty grand in the bank pretty rich," Rafe said.

Cassidy saw Jace's head snap around as he stared at the other man rather too pointedly to just be a response to him speaking. "Yes," he said. "There are."

There had been something in those words, too, something harsh and…personal? Whatever it was, she didn't like it. Jace had had enough of that in his life, with his strict, overbearing father. The man had made her feel impossibly inadequate the few times she'd been around him, and Cory had told her tales that had made her shudder, so she could only imagine how he'd made Jace feel.

"I don't think my brother could be involved in this. I haven't spoken to him in several weeks, and I haven't seen him in four months," she said now. She glanced at Jace. "I did try to call him a few times before I called you. He never called back."

"Sounds par for the course for him."

She sighed. "It didn't used to be."

"A lot of things didn't used to be."

Again that edge had crept into his voice. And this time he was facing her, and she saw him fight it down.

"He's the one who left me your number and told me…to call you if I couldn't reach him and needed help. Because you—"

She cut herself off, realizing they were into territory she wasn't sure she wanted to discuss in front of a complete stranger, even one who was here to help.

"Made him a promise," Jace finished softly.

"Yes."

"And that promise," the man she'd been worried about talking in front of said, "is why Foxworth is involved. Helping good people keep honest promises is high on the list of things we do."

It seemed impossible to her that such a thing existed, yet here they were, this intimidating man who looked as if he'd have no problem handling any trouble that came at him, and the dog who somehow made him less frightening.

"Speaking of lists," he added, "I'll need one, of everyone you see on a regular basis. The personal names first, then business. Include when you last saw or spoke to them, and the circumstances. Don't try to narrow it down, or leave anyone off that you think is unlikely or impossible. Let us do that."

"Us?" She glanced at Jace, who hadn't been in her life for nearly ten years. Never mind that he'd often been in her mind.

"I meant Foxworth," Rafe said. "We've got resources."

She frowned. "And you're going to use them to, what? Poke around in the lives of everyone I know?"

"I promise you, they will never know."

She still didn't like the idea. "I don't think so."

For a brief moment, he didn't answer. He looked just rueful enough that her entire impression of him changed. In that moment he looked like a man in unknown waters. It echoed in his voice when he said, "I made a big assumption, Ms. Grant, and I shouldn't have."

"What big assumption?"

He nodded. "That you wanted our help. I'm not usually the front man for Foxworth, or I wouldn't have forgotten a crucial step."

"What are you, usually?"

Surprise flickered in his eyes, but only for an instant. "If I answered that, you might say no when you need to say yes."

She wasn't sure what to make of that but guessed he meant that if there was dirty work to be done, he did it. She wasn't really certain what that would be, but if they got involved in things like this, what else might they deal with? For a moment she questioned whether she did indeed want the help being offered.

The dog at her knee shifted, drawing her gaze. Dark, amber-flecked eyes looked up into hers, and she felt suddenly steadier. And certain that it was all right. *How odd.*

She looked back at Rafe, who didn't speak again, didn't try to persuade her, just let her process. She studied him for a moment longer, then said quietly, "I think whatever the situation, I would want you on my side and not against me."

Rafe smiled. It was not, she thought, a happy smile.

"Told you she was smart," Jace said.

Cassidy's gaze shifted to him as she wondered what else he'd told the man. And she caught him watching her with the oddest expression on his face.

"You still have the scar," she said, rather inanely. Of course he still had it.

He lifted a hand as if instinctively, to touch the mark below his eye. "My favorite souvenir."

She felt a faint heat rising in her cheeks. "Something to remind you of a silly girl you had to rescue?"

"You were never silly. And I never needed the scar for that."

His voice was so soft, so gentle, yet with that rough edge he'd gained somewhere in the last ten years. His words set up a chain reaction of memories, hopes that she'd thought successfully quashed for good. She was afraid the pink in her face would turn to full red if she didn't look away. So she quickly did, only to find Rafe Crawford watching them both thoughtfully.

But thankfully the man said nothing except, "That list? And a schedule, too. Where you usually are when, and what days might vary and why."

That, at least she could see the reason for. And so, wondering on several fronts what she'd gotten herself into, she went to the kitchen drawer where she kept stray notepads and began to write.

Chapter 5

"You could have mentioned she was more to you than your friend's sister," Rafe said casually, quietly.

Jace felt a jolt at the words and with a touch of panic tried to gauge if Cassie could have heard him over there in the kitchen. She never faltered in her writing, so he guessed not. Then he looked back at Rafe and realized this was a man who would know exactly how far his voice would or would not carry.

"She's not," he said. *At least, she wasn't.* "I mean, I liked her, enough to tease her a lot. Like she was my sister, too. Cory said she…kind of had a crush on me. You know, the kind of thing that happens with teenage girls."

"She's not a teenage girl now."

Jace glanced at her. "No kidding. I never thought she'd grow up like…that."

"Nothing sisterly about her now."

Jace swallowed tightly. "No. No, not a thing."

"Except that promise."

His gaze shot back to Rafe's face. "Yeah. That promise."

He'd made that promise to Cory, to take care of his

sister if ever he couldn't. To look out for her, help her if she needed it.

"Doesn't sound like her brother's the type to keep them."

"Depends how much it costs him." The rather cynical observation was out before he thought. His mouth tightened ruefully. What was it about this guy—and that blessed dog—that made him say things he normally would never say? Especially to someone he'd just met?

"Some would say that lets you off the hook."

Jace's brow furrowed. "Why? I made the promise, not Cory."

The slightest of smiles flitted across the other man's face. "And that you make that distinction is why I'm here. You're the kind of person Foxworth helps. Cory, not so much."

Jace was saved from responding by Cassie's return. She handed Rafe the list of names. "You swear they won't ever know?"

"As long as they're not involved in whatever this is, they won't have a clue," Rafe promised. Somehow Jace thought the guy would deliver on that.

"And if they are?" she asked, warily. "If someone on this list—" she sounded extremely doubtful "—turns out to be my stalker, what then?"

"That's up to you," Rafe answered.

"Me? Not...the police?"

Rafe gave a one-shouldered shrug. "We work with the police, often. They like us because we share what we can, sometimes things they don't know. If it becomes a police matter, we cooperate. And if it turns into something big for them, we don't want the credit. But we're not bound by their rules, which sometimes cripple them. And we work for you."

Cassie still looked uncertain. Jace couldn't really blame her; he'd seen the Foxworth setup, had watched as Rafe had started certain wheels in motion, and he still couldn't quite believe it all.

"Think of it like this," Rafe suggested. "Imagine finding out it's a friend with a misguided but innocent reason. That would make you feel differently than if it's some unbalanced stranger with a fixation."

"Oh." She grimaced. "Yes. I see what you mean."

"If it is that…stranger," Jace began.

"Then we'll deal," Rafe said. "I'll get the process of elimination started with our tech guy. But there's one more thing. We all need to be clear on what the goal is here."

"Keep Cassie safe," Jace said instantly.

"Catch him," Cassie said simultaneously.

Startled, Jace stared at her. "Cassie," he began.

She looked at Rafe as if for support. "The one accomplishes the other, right?"

"Yes," Rafe agreed, "but I'd say Jace's goal has to come first. Your safety is paramount."

"Exactly," Jace agreed. And he was suddenly relieved that they had this man on their side, to accomplish just that. But then Rafe spoke again and blasted all other thoughts out of his head.

"So Jace should stay here with you. Just seeing you're not alone should slow this guy down."

Cassie frowned. Which made Jace frown and refocus. Was the idea of him under her roof that distasteful? Did she—

"But won't that just make him wait?" she asked, snapping him back to reality, where it seemed the idea of him under her roof didn't matter at all. And he wasn't sure that didn't bother him even more.

Feeling suddenly contrary, Jace said, "If I stay long enough, he'll move on, won't he?"

"Depends on his goal," Rafe said. Then, sounding almost weary, he added, "Some fixations can withstand both time and logic."

Cassie studied the other man for a moment. Then, quietly, she said, "You've dealt with this kind of thing before, then."

"Yes. Foxworth has dealt with several stalking cases."

"I mean you, personally."

Again the shrug. "Three."

"And how did they end up?" Jace asked.

"One misunderstanding. One in jail." He stopped.

"And the third?" Cassie prompted.

Jace watched Rafe meet her gaze. "Dead."

If the Foxworth man had thought she would crumple, he'd misjudged her. Jace hadn't. He knew Cassidy Grant was made of sterner stuff than that. Still, he stayed silent, curious to see how she responded.

"Since I doubt you're the type to indiscriminately kill, I presume it was necessary."

Rafe's voice was barely above a whisper. "There are some who would say I'm exactly that type."

Jace had the sudden feeling this was about something else entirely. And that if this man had killed, as he'd said, it was not something he did lightly. And he would carry the responsibility of it forever. Jace was certain of it in the same way he was certain that his father was the most irresponsible man on the planet, if indeed he still was on it.

For the first time since he'd taken a position at Cassie's side, the dog moved. He padded silently over to the man with the haunted eyes and nudged his hand. And again without a look, with the appearance of a habit long ingrained, Rafe put his hand on the dog's head.

"Thanks, buddy," he murmured. "I'm okay."

Jace glanced at Cassie, who was watching the pair intently.

"All right," she said suddenly. "What else do you need me to do?"

"Go about your business. Jace, stay close."

"And you?" Jace asked.

"I'll be around. Never far."

"I only have one guest room, but there's a foldout couch in—"

She stopped as Rafe shook his head. "I need to be outside. Able to move."

"But at night—" Cassie began to protest.

"At night most of all."

Jace was hit with a sudden certainty that under cover of night, this man could be one of the deadliest predators that walked.

"It's November. It's cold at night," Cassie protested.

Rafe smiled at her. "I'll survive."

"And it won't be the first time, will it?" Jace asked, already knowing the answer.

"Nor likely the last," Rafe said, meeting his gaze. Then, in the tone of someone used to thinking in such ways, he said, "He'll be checking you out, assessing."

Jace nodded. "How should I play it? Tough or wimp?"

Rafe grinned, and Jace felt oddly as if he'd won some sort of award. "In between, I think. Let him wonder. Who you are, and how capable you are." He gave Cassie a glance that looked apologetic. "We can't be absolutely certain he doesn't at least know your brother, so I don't think that pretense would work."

"Bodyguard?" Jace asked.

"That implies training and will make him more cautious," Rafe said. He glanced from him to Cassie. "Boyfriend, I think, if you can pull it off."

Jace groaned inwardly. Then he nearly frowned, because he didn't understand why he'd reacted on such a gut level to what was a logical solution.

"But if he's been watching me, won't he know I don't have one?" Cassie asked, apparently unruffled by the idea.

"You're sure it's only been three weeks?" Rafe asked.

"I think so. But like I said, I might not have realized it right away."

"I'm guessing you picked up on it pretty quickly. Say, maybe three days of seeing him repeatedly at the most. So we'll go with three weeks."

"Which means?" Jace asked.

"He wasn't around when we got here today. He could

be watching from a distance, but if he is, he won't be sure what's going on. For all he knows, I just picked your boyfriend up at the airport after a trip somewhere that started just about when he started watching you."

"So we're having a joyous reunion," Jace said. He kept his voice carefully even, but he heard a tiny sound from Cassie, as if she'd only just realized what this was going to involve. "Together every minute because I've been gone."

"Something like that, yes," Rafe agreed.

"I don't know…" Cassie began before Jace turned to her.

"You can do it, Cassie." He managed a wry grin. "Just look at me like you did when you were sixteen."

He saw her stiffen, draw herself up. Ah, there was the Cassie he remembered, quiet but strong.

"Oh, I wasn't worried about that." Her tone was as light as her posture was determined. "I can make cow eyes at you just like I used to. I was more worried about you, pretending to look at me like that."

"I'll manage."

And he would. All too easily.

He was just going to have to be careful it didn't become real.

Cassidy was feeling a little like a spoiled child. She'd been scared, had wanted help, had called for help and now that it was here, she was unhappy about it.

I just never expected he would move in, and we'd have to pretend to be…lovers.

The very thought made her shiver and reminded her

too sharply of the days and nights when she had pined after Jace with all the longing of an infatuated teenage heart. And that moment when he'd said he bought flowers for his mom, and she'd felt a jab of cheer that he hadn't mentioned a girlfriend.

She distracted herself by studying the cell phone Rafe had given her, a twin to the one he'd given Jace, after she'd explained why she'd been afraid to use hers.

"He may not be savvy enough to hack your phone, but it can't hurt. But we need communications," he'd said and gone out to his car and opened the trunk. When he came back, he'd had the two phones. "They're Foxworth," he'd explained as he showed them how they worked. "And as unhackable as a phone can be. They also function as a direct connection, so if anything happens I need to know, or if you're in trouble, you've got one-button contact."

Somehow this man saying it made it seem more real than even that night when the shadow outside her bedroom window had so terrified her.

They'd then spent another hour going over things she never would have even thought might be connected. The business, finances, other relatives, even any lingering threads from her parents' deaths.

"I've got some things to check," Rafe finally said. He looked at Jace. "You've got first watch. Stay with her, keep that phone handy and don't hesitate to use it. I'll call you when I take over, then you can get some rest."

"What about you?" Cassidy asked.

"Don't worry about me," Rafe said and headed for the back door she'd shown him earlier. Cassidy wondered who did worry about him. "I'm going to check around outside first. Cutter, with me."

The dog spun on his hind legs and was at Rafe's side in a single leap. Gone was the quiet, gentle, soothing animal she'd seen so far; this was a working dog now, and the difference was startling. Dog and man made an impressive team, and yet again the word that occurred to her was *intimidating*.

And then they were gone, so quietly she wasn't certain at first that they hadn't just stayed on the back deck.

"Wow," she said, a little taken aback. "You really called in the cavalry."

"Ex, maybe," Jace agreed. "But I told you, he found me. Well, the dog did."

She smiled at that. "Not sure what I think of that dog. He's almost spooky, the way he seems to sense things."

"Rafe says he still surprises them all the time. At home he patrols the neighborhood twice a day, and last month he stole the cell phone of a neighbor so she'd come after him, because she had a problem Foxworth could help her with."

Cassidy blinked. "And just how did he know that?"

"No idea."

"Have you looked them up?"

"No." His mouth twisted again. "No phone, remember? But we stopped at their office on the way here. Pretty impressive setup. They've even got a helicopter, and apparently a small plane at the local airfield."

"Fancy place?"

"No, not at all. Kind of hidden in the trees, not even a sign. Rafe says they work mostly by word of mouth. And lately, the dog." She laughed. Jace shrugged. "Yeah. Sounds crazy, but here I am."

A sudden warmth filled her. Yes, he was. She'd called, and he'd come. Just like he'd promised. "You're still a good guy, Jace Robinson."

He'd been looking at the new phone, but now his head came up sharply. "Not Robinson. Not anymore."

Cassidy blinked. "What?"

"I don't use…his name anymore."

For a moment she just stared at him, unsure what, if anything, she should say to that. She'd always known he and his father didn't get along and suspected from some things both her parents and Cory had said that he wasn't a pleasant guy. And then Jace had started taking judo lessons with Cory, and she'd wondered again if there was more to it than just a guy's fascination with martial arts. But then he'd started winning competitions, and he rarely mentioned his father anyway, so she'd kind of forgotten.

"Okay," she finally said, knowing she sounded rather lame but unable to think of anything else to say.

"That's it? 'Okay'?" He looked at her steadily, as if daring her to question him.

She kept her voice even. "I assume you had good reason. From what little I knew of your father, I think I understand."

He let out a breath, relaxing a little, and she wondered what others had assumed. That he was some career criminal looking for a new start, or some victim of media overreach looking for anonymity?

"I had it legally changed when my mom went back to her maiden name, Cahill."

"So you're Jace Cahill now?"

He nodded.

"Sounds good together," she said, meaning it. She left it at that. "By whatever name, thank you for coming. I feel a little silly now. It sounds so crazy when I say it to someone else—" She stopped when he held up a hand.

"I'm sure most stalking victims think it sounds crazy until they find out it's true. And better you take steps and it turns out not to be anything than not and it does. Or something." He gave her that crooked smile that had always sent her pulse racing. It still did, and she looked down, a little embarrassed that after all this time he could have this effect on her.

She supposed she shouldn't be. He had the same bright blue eyes and that same sweetly crooked smile. His body was still tall and lean, and he still had that way of shoving one hand in his jeans pocket that made her hyperaware of the lean maleness of his hips. The fact that he looked older now, a bit older even than she knew he was, only made him more attractive. True, he looked a bit careworn, his hair longer and a bit shaggy, his jeans frayed and faded, his jacket torn on one side, his boots worn and with what looked like a strip of duct tape across one toe. Then again, people paid lots of money for just that look in a futile effort to appear cool.

But that kind of guy didn't travel over a thousand miles to keep a silly promise to look out for his friend's younger sister.

"Let's get you settled in," she said, making an effort

at sounding brisk and efficient, and succeeding somewhat. "Are you hungry?"

"Starved," he admitted with a rueful twist of his mouth.

"Then aren't you lucky I made spaghetti sauce yesterday," she said lightly.

As if on cue his stomach growled. And it made his protest that she didn't have to do that sound like exactly what it was, a token.

"You came all this way to help me, the least I can do is feed you." She led him down the hall. He glanced at a doorway as they passed—Cory's old room. "It's still Cory's," she said, "not that he uses it anymore. He just stores a lot of junk in there. I can't get him to clean it out."

"I still remember those bunk beds your dad built. I always thought that was so cool. Not just the beds, but that he built them himself."

He had always liked them, she remembered. And she remembered his reaction when he'd first looked at the footboards her father had carved. *Hey, wings!* Cory had looked at him blankly, even her father had seemed puzzled, but she had seen what he meant—the angle of the design did look like seagull wings.

"He was a very handy guy," she said softly.

"I'm sorry," Jace said. "I didn't mean to bring up painful memories."

"They're not painful," she assured him quickly. "I love that people remember him like that. Most people don't talk about them, and it feels like they've forgotten they ever existed."

They'd reached the door to the guest room. "I moved into the master," she said. "After a year or so. It seemed silly not to, if I was going to keep the place."

Funny, when she'd decided to move back into this house after her parents had been killed in that accident, she'd thought she would find it too big, too full of memories for her to ever relax. And yet she'd found it strangely comforting.

"Only makes sense," he said. "And you've made it yours."

"I've tried." She had redone many things, added her own touch.

"Besides, it's not like being somewhere else is going to stop the memories. They're in you. Places just trigger them."

She stared at him. "Yes. Exactly."

It wasn't that she was surprised; Jace had always had depth to him. One of those memories he'd just mentioned flashed into her mind, of her sixteen-year-old self saying to her mother how much more mature—that was a popular word to her then—he seemed than Cory.

"He is," her mother had said, a touch of sadness in her voice. "His father is…a difficult man."

She had wondered for an instant if the sadness was for Jace or that Cory wasn't as mature. Decided it had to be for Jace, because she was sure Cory would eventually catch up. She'd been wrong about that, but at the time she'd been certain.

"But his mom's so sweet," she'd said.

"Yes. Which makes it even more difficult."

She hadn't understood then. But when her father had

come home with the news that Jace and his mother had moved away because his father had left them, she thought she did.

"Can I ask you something?" she said when they were in the guest room, he'd dropped his worn pack on the bed and she'd shown him where clean towels were.

"You can always ask," he said.

Doesn't mean I'll answer. She heard what he didn't say but went ahead. "When your mom moved away, you were… eighteen." He nodded, giving her a curious look. "I was just wondering…you had that job at the lumberyard, and your friends here…" She trailed off awkwardly.

"You mean why did I go with her?"

"Yes."

He leaned against the small dresser, crossing his ankles and his arms. Defensively? she wondered. "Thinking I was a mama's boy who couldn't be away from her?"

Yes, definitely defensively. "I never thought that. Ever."

He let out an audible breath. "She needed help. I couldn't just walk away."

"Especially after your father did."

His gaze narrowed. "You know that, then."

She smiled apologetically. "I'm afraid the whole neighborhood did."

He grimaced. "I figured."

"We all knew your dad was…"

"An assh—"

He cut himself off. She found herself wondering if

he'd done it to avoid being foul in front of her, or if he really didn't like calling his father crude names, even if they fit. Either way, it only made her more certain Jace Rob—Cahill was exactly the guy she remembered. The good guy she remembered.

Unfortunately, she thought as she left him to get settled, that also meant he was still the guy she'd had her first-ever serious crush on. The guy whose thick-lashed eyes had stirred her to sighs, and whose lean, broad-shouldered body had caused feelings in her she hadn't even recognized. The guy all others since had had to measure up to, and usually failed.

And from what she'd seen—and felt—so far, that hadn't changed a bit.

Chapter 6

Jace listened to her footsteps as she went back down the hall. He was feeling a little off balance, here in this house where he'd spent many hours as a kid. It had been a revelation to him then, that not all parents fought constantly, that in some homes, children were appreciated and encouraged by their father, not a nuisance to be rid of as often as possible.

I didn't mean to break it, Mr. Grant, really. Please...

His own heartfelt plea as he stood over the shards of the flower pot he'd inadvertently shattered with the baseball he and Cory had been tossing. Cory had told him to burn it in and he had, but Cory had panicked at the last second and dodged away.

He remembered cringing when Cory's father had crouched before him.

I know you didn't, Jace. It's all right. It was an accident. Come on in, have some lunch.

He remembered the shock that had filled him at that moment, that not only was Mr. Grant not going to scream curses at him, but that he was still welcome in his house.

Remembered even more the look in the man's eyes, the look he hated and only later had come to recognize as pity.

A wave of weariness swept over him, and he sat on the edge of the bed. It had been a long haul just to get here, and he was afraid Rafe might have been a bit optimistic about him being able to stay awake until he took over. He wondered what the guy was doing, suspected it had something to do with that industrial-strength laptop he'd seen in the car that looked like it could withstand a direct hit from a hand grenade.

The urge to lie down, just for a moment, nearly swamped him. But he was afraid if he did he would be asleep before he hit the pillow.

You've got first watch.

Damn, that made it sound so real. He'd known Cassie was scared, but it hadn't really seemed possible that she was in real danger until Rafe had said that. He was taking this very seriously, and given his demeanor and that look in his eyes, Jace guessed he knew what he was talking about.

He stood up abruptly before that pillow could lure him in. He opened his pack and started pulling out what was there. He'd packed light, so there wasn't much, and what there was needed washing after the long trek. Maybe he could do that here, if Cassie didn't mind.

It hit him then, and his head came up. He looked around the room. The walls were a neutral cream, with splashes of green and blue—the throw pillow on the chair, the vase on the dresser and the geometric pattern of the comforter on the bed. But in his mind's eye it was a pale green, with white shelves on that wall, full of books almost to the ceiling. And that silly, droopy stuffed dog on the top shelf. He'd always thought of him as standing guard over her precious books.

Belatedly what she had meant when she'd talked of moving into the master bedroom registered. This had been Cassie's room. He'd only seen it a couple of times, and that had been from down the hall at Cory's room, when the door happened to be open. And once when he'd come out and caught her peeking out into the hallway, as if to see if anyone was around. When she'd seen him, she'd gasped and darted back inside and closed the door.

That was the first time he'd thought maybe Cory was right about Cassie having a crush on him.

It felt odd—maybe downright weird—to be in this room now. True, it was totally different now, down to the color, but it still nagged at him.

He caught a whiff of some luscious scent that his stomach quickly registered as food and a second later his mind labeled spaghetti sauce. It wiped all else from his mind, and he headed down the hall.

Cassie was putting a foil-wrapped bundle in the oven. She glanced at him. "You mind garlic?"

"Only if there's not enough," he said, sucking in a deep breath of the great smells.

She laughed and shut the oven door. "In about fifteen, then."

"Great. Thank you."

She just smiled at him, and he felt an odd sort of tumble inside.

"While I was stirring, I looked up Foxworth," she said. "It seems they're quite something."

She nodded toward the tablet that lay on the counter. He picked it up and looked at the website she had open. It was slick, streamlined, and had all the basics. Contact info for the five locations Rafe had mentioned, although no addresses. A short bio of the namesakes of the Foundation, Rafe's boss's parents. Some effusively grateful testimonials, clearly written by people who had been at the end of their rope.

And not much more. In fact, it seemed to him that if you didn't already know what they did, you'd never know what they did.

"It doesn't really say what they do," she said, echoing his thought.

"Rafe said they work mostly by word of mouth. And the dog." She laughed again. He looked at her. "It's good to hear you laugh."

"I wasn't," she said ruefully, "until you got here. But I feel much better now."

"Worth the trip, then," he said, ignoring the fact that he wasn't at all sure he was going to be able to help. But he was fairly sure Rafe knew what he was doing, so maybe he had helped, indirectly. Or the dog had.

"That's so sad, about the guy's parents dying in that terrorist attack."

"What inspired the whole thing, Rafe said. They turned it into something good. Kind of like you keeping the family business going."

She sighed. "Not what I'd pictured myself doing, but I couldn't just let it go."

He remembered what she'd told him with heartfelt earnestness when she'd been about fourteen. "You wanted to travel the country, see all the places you'd read about."

She looked startled. "You remember that?"

"Sure." *I understood. I wanted to be anywhere but here.*

Then, it had only been the desire to escape. But now running off with Cassidy Grant took on an entirely different meaning.

Whoa. He almost took a step back. This sudden awareness of her, as not his best friend's little sister, but of the woman she was now, had him completely off-kilter.

"I guess we don't always get what we want," she said, and she gave him a sideways glance.

He had the strangest feeling she was talking about him, or at least the kid she'd once had a crush on. Then he told himself he was only thinking that because of the crazy direction his own thoughts had veered into.

"Could I borrow your washing machine?" he asked, rather abruptly, trying to snap his weird train of thought.

"Of course. If you need something to wear while you wash your things, Cory has some stuff in the closet in his room." She wrinkled her nose. "If you can get to it past all the other stuff in there."

"I climbed two-thirds of Mount Rainier once. I'll manage."

She stared at him. "You did?"

He nodded. "When I was sixteen. Made it to Camp Muir at ten thousand feet."

"Wait, I remember Cory talking about that. It was a school trip, wasn't it? I can't remember why he didn't go."

"He did, he just didn't make the upper climb."

He didn't mention that they'd had to qualify to go beyond the easier reaches, and Cory had skipped the training classes. Jace hadn't missed one, because it got him out of the house and away from his father on the weekends.

"I wanted to do that, but I was too young," she said with a sigh.

"You would have, too." He meant it. Even then she had had that kind of spirit and the drive that her brother lacked.

He went back to the bedroom to empty dirty clothes out of his backpack. He was nearly done when he heard a noise from outside. His first thought was Rafe, but he dismissed it immediately; the guy never made noise, and he'd be willing to bet—if he ever bet—that Cutter didn't, either. He could hear Cassie in the kitchen, and he knew the door there was locked. And the noise he'd heard had come from the side nearest this room.

He edged over to the window, trying to see outside without moving the curtain. He waited, listening intently. Heard it again—the faintest of scrapes, like something over concrete. Not close to the house, but no farther than the fence, he guessed.

His mind raced. He could go out into the dark and try to catch whoever—or possibly whatever—it was. Or he could flip on the outside lights and let him know he'd been heard.

Keep Cassie safe.

Catch him.

Their simultaneous answers echoed in his head. And

his decision still held; keeping Cassie safe was paramount.

He dropped everything on the bed, spun and headed for the bedroom door. Cassie looked up, startled, as he belted through the dining room to the back door. He hit the light switch with one hand and unlocked and yanked open the door with the other. He was outside before a second ticked down.

The backyard and patio were empty. Looked exactly as they had before. He wondered if his imagination had been playing tricks on him. But he did a careful walk around anyway.

"Jace?" Cassie's voice sounded worried as she called out from the back door.

"Go back in. I'll be there in a minute."

She hesitated, and he hoped she wasn't going to argue, not this moment. Because he'd just spotted something. "Hurry," she said and went back inside.

Breathing again, he walked toward the corner of the house where Cassie's old room was. Everything looked fine. Except for that one oddity he'd spotted: a branch of the small maple tree next to the fence, now bare of the fall-bright leaves it had likely had just a couple of weeks ago, was now caught at an unnatural angle over the top of the fence.

The light from the patio cast everything into stark relief, making the shadows seem even darker. Nothing else looked amiss. He searched the ground around the tree and saw nothing unexpected. He crossed the last couple of feet to the fence, reached up to grasp the top and hoisted himself up for a look over.

He hadn't been imagining it. Because out in the alley, up against the fence, was a stack of wooden pallets. Pallets he'd noticed earlier behind her neighbor's garage. Now placed on top of each other in exactly the spot where he'd heard the noise. And right where somebody trying to see or even climb over that fence might get tangled up with that maple branch.

Cassie hadn't been imagining things, either. And that sent his stomach into a plummeting free fall.

It was real.

They were nearly through the meal that Jace thought was the best thing he'd had in weeks. Cassie had eaten, but not much, and he thought she was much more rattled by the proof he'd found that her suspicions were true than she was letting show. And he couldn't think of anything to say to her that was reassuring. "You were right but we'll catch him" didn't seem quite right.

The cell phone Rafe had given him let out a buzz. It was clearly different from a normal ring, so he picked it up and pressed the red intercom button.

"I've got it outside now," the man said without preamble. "Get some sleep."

Jace glanced at the time readout on the oven across from him. It was 9:00 p.m. now, so he did some quick math. "When should I relieve you? One?"

"I'm good for tonight. You need to stick with her in daylight hours."

Quickly, Jace told him what he'd heard and found by the fence. "Explains why Cutter was revved up when we got back here," Rafe said.

"Any sign of anything else?" he asked, assuming he probably knew the answer or Rafe would have led with that.

"Not current. But somebody's been around. Cutter verified my guess it was recent."

His breath caught in his throat again. Yes, this was all definitely real.

"Right. All right. I'll be up before first light."

"Not saying much up here."

"Oh. Yeah." Jace felt foolish, now that he remembered sunrise here this time of year was about seven thirty. "I forgot. Five, then. What I'm used to."

When he put down the phone, he found Cassie watching him.

"You're used to getting up at 5:00 a.m.? What happened to the guy who liked to stay up late and sleep in?"

She said it lightly, but it still stung. The memory of staying up late because they were the only hours he had without his father bit at him. "Reality," he snapped.

He saw his sharp tone register, and he sighed inwardly. He was about to mutter a "sorry" when she smiled rather ruefully. "Bites all of us eventually, I think."

"Yeah." It was then he saw the chance to say something that had been nagging at him for years. He hesitated, not wanting to bring back unpleasant memories, but then he realized they were probably never far away anyway, for Cassie. "I really was sorry about your folks. I felt terrible that I couldn't get here for the funeral. They were always so good to me."

"They liked you. A lot."

And he had liked them. Her father had become his

model of what a parent should be, since his own had been such a disaster. And so he'd in fact felt like utter crap not being able to get here. At the time he couldn't afford a plane ticket, or the time away from work. Hell, he still couldn't afford it, hence the bus ride and hitchhiking.

Back then he'd been in a lousy mood for days, until his quiet, gentle mother had sat him down and demanded to know what was wrong. He was bad-tempered enough at that point to tell her and then instantly regretted it when she'd nearly cried.

You're doing this for me, and—

I'm doing it because one male in this family should be responsible, damn it.

"Sometime," Cassie said softly, yanking him out of the painful memory, "will you tell me what happened?"

He looked at her, at the same time aware of the house he was standing in, that nice, well-tended, spacious place like the one down the street he'd spent his first years in. Compared it to the tiny, old and very shabby apartments he and his mother had lived in until just this last summer when he'd finally moved her into a nice place.

"Not likely," he muttered.

This time she didn't smile. "I see." She looked hurt.

Nice work, Cahill. You've been in her house maybe three hours, and you've already hurt her feelings. Twice.

He hadn't intended that. But then, he seemed to have the knack to upset women, so maybe he should have expected it.

Then again, given his weird reaction to her, maybe some distance was a good idea. She'd become the hottest thing he'd been close to in a long time, but he was here to help her, not lust after her.

They finished the meal in a silence that wasn't quite strained but certainly wasn't the pleasant way they'd started, even with the discovery he'd made outside hanging over them. He helped her clean up after, during which the only conversation was about the task at hand.

In a very businesslike manner she showed him the laundry room and told him to have at it. Still regretting having hurt her feelings, while facing the fact that he was in no way ready to talk about what his life had become since they'd left town, he ventured into Cory's old room.

She hadn't been kidding—there was stuff piled everywhere, and some of it made him step carefully. But he managed to dig a pair of sweatpants out of a bottom drawer. They would do while he was washing his own stuff, he thought.

He took a shower, quick and merely warm because he didn't know what the hot water situation was. Then he pulled on the sweats. He was a little taller than Cory, but also leaner, so that made up for the length. They were a bit loose, so he tightened the drawstring a little, then grabbed up his clothes from the floor. He walked back to the guest room—Cassie's old room—added the ones from the pack to his pile and dumped them all in the washing machine. They'd all been washed so often he didn't worry about anything fading; they were already there.

When the machine was going, he turned to leave the compact but workable laundry space. And nearly ran into Cassie, who was standing in the doorway.

She was staring at him. And blushing.

Instinctively he glanced down, thinking he hadn't pulled that drawstring tight enough. But while they were riding a little low, the essentials were still covered. And it wasn't like Cassie hadn't seen his bare chest before. True, it had been years ago, but still...

"I just thought...without a phone...you might need this. I moved it out of that room to the living room when that one died, but it can go back for now." Only then did he realize she was holding a small electric alarm clock. "It doesn't take up much room on the nightstand. I know you're more of a play-it-by-ear kind of guy, but—"

"Not anymore," he said, thinking it sounded almost like she was nervous. She didn't usually jabber, and that's what that flood of words sounded like. "Thanks."

He took the clock. Odd, that little jolt as their fingers touched. It had been raining far too much for any static electricity to be lingering. But she pulled her hand back as if she'd felt it, too. He was still pondering it as he walked into the guest room, plugged the clock in, set the time and put it on the nightstand.

Yes, his days of dealing with time casually were long over.

Cassidy leaned against her closed bedroom door, breathing easily for maybe the first time since Jace had appeared on her doorstep. She wanted to close her eyes, but she didn't dare, because she knew perfectly well if she did all she would see was that image of him, half-naked, Cory's sweats slung low on his hips. That broad, strong chest, the flat, ribbed abdomen, the lean hips... he looked like an escapee from a fitness magazine.

Apparently even as a kid she'd had good taste, because he was still the most beautiful thing she'd ever seen. And she didn't need to close her eyes, apparently, because it was playing back in her mind as vividly as if she were still standing there, gaping at him.

So much for breathing easy.

If she kept this up, he was going to be very sorry he'd come to help. And she'd best remember that was the only reason he was here—because she'd made that panicked phone call. If he'd wanted to come on his own, he'd always known where she was. Jace was here to keep a promise he'd made, probably never expecting it to be called in. It would be very shabby of her to start drooling on him.

She heard a dog bark and for a second wondered if it was Cutter. But she instantly discarded the thought; that yippy sound had never issued from that dog's throat. More likely it was Mrs. Alston's little terrier, down at the end of the block toward the thick grove of trees they'd played in as kids, where the old cabin was.

Next door to Jace's old house.

And there she was, right back at the subject she was trying so very hard to avoid.

She bustled about, getting ready for bed with much more concentration than the task required, or than she normally gave it. She had the rueful thought that her life could never be normal with Jace just down the hall.

It was a long night, without much sleep accomplished. And she was up even before Jace, who, true to his word, was up at five. She knew, because she heard the faint creak of the floorboard just inside the door of that bedroom, a creak she knew all too well from when it had been her room and she'd tried to sneak out without her parents knowing.

When she was dressed, she went out and put coffee on. She was going to need it. A lot of it. A glance down the hall had told her the light was on in the guest room—she determinedly thought of it that way, not as her room, and spared a moment to be thankful she'd replaced her old, rather girly white bedroom set with something more neutral, since the idea of Jace sleeping in what had once been her bed was far too unsettling, no matter that she hadn't slept in it in years, and God, even her thoughts were rambling now...

Thankfully, when Jace came out, he was fully dressed in jeans and a long-sleeved henley shirt. They both looked a bit worse for wear, but they were now freshly washed. She thought again of how people paid a lot of money to buy jeans that looked exactly like those, worn and broken in. But she'd be willing to bet Jace's were that way genuinely, that he'd earned every hole and fray.

He was unshaven, which she didn't mind, his hair thoroughly tousled, which she liked, and his bright blue eyes a little bloodshot. As if he'd slept no better than she had. And she wasn't at all sure how she felt about that.

He gestured with the Foxworth phone as he set it on the bar. "Rafe buzzed as soon as the light came on. He said he's going to head over to the shop to make sure it's clear, but he's sending Cutter back here."

Cassidy blinked. "He's sending the dog back?"

Jace nodded, rubbing a hand over his jaw. "He said he's got the scent of the guy now, so he'll alert if he's around."

She must be more tired than she thought. "He's sending the dog back, alone, to a house he's been in exactly once?"

Jace gave her a crooked smile. It was the one she'd fallen for like a ton of mulch as a kid, except now it was…sexier. Or she knew enough now to classify it that way. She tamped down the crazy reaction. "I get the feeling he's a lot smarter than the average dog."

"You mean like Max?" she asked, remembering the lovable but a bit dim mutt he'd had as a child. "Poor baby."

Jace had gone very still.

"I'm sorry," she said quickly. "I know how hard it was for you when he got killed by that car. He was so sweet. Accidents like that are so horrible."

"It wasn't," he said tightly, "an accident."

"What?"

"And the car was my father's."

She stared at him. "Are you saying…he hit him on purpose?"

"He did."

"But…why?"

"Because I loved him. And one day he growled at my father when he was shouting at me."

She couldn't breathe. She knew his father had been a hard, harsh man, but this… She couldn't think of a thing to say. And he was already looking like he regretted telling her.

She was saved by a faint, very polite bark at her back door. Grateful for the interruption, she hurried over and pulled the door open. Cutter was indeed sitting there, looking up at her, for all the world as if he were waiting to be invited inside. She couldn't resist reaching out to pat his dark head.

"Well, hello, Mr. Cutter. Please come in. So glad you could make it."

The dog whuffed softly as he trotted in, and Cassidy found herself laughingly thinking it sounded like a thank-you. He walked over to Jace, who appeared to have recovered from letting the grim truth slip out, and nudged his hand. She saw him let out a breath before he reached to scratch behind the dog's right ear. Cutter leaned into him as if that was his favorite touch ever, and she made note of that. If the dog was going to be around, it would be good to know.

She busied herself for a moment, putting a towel on the floor in the kitchen and setting a bowl of water on top of it. The dog lapped up a bit, then plopped down beside the bowl and watched them.

"Not sure what I have for you for breakfast," she said to the animal. "Bacon? Some ham, maybe. Kind of salty, though."

"Rafe said he already fed him. He's good to go with us."

She looked up at Jace. "Go with…us?"

"To the shop. You open at nine, right?"

"Yes, although I try to get there by eight to do paperwork and tidy up. But you—"

"Will be right there."

"You don't have to do that. I'll be fine there."

"You don't know that. This started with him hanging around outside the shop."

"Well, yes, but he's never come in."

"Now likely he never will," Jace said, gesturing at

the dog she guessed could be intimidating if he chose to be. "Rafe will watch the shop until we get there to be sure it's clear."

"But what if he just waits? You can't…stay forever."

She had hesitated when she realized how her words would sound. Been startled at the sudden longing that blossomed inside her when she said them. And now wondered if she imagined that slight pause before he gave her that grin again.

"I'm sure you wouldn't want that. But Rafe says we'll get this guy wrapped up and you'll get your life back."

"And when does he sleep?" she asked, looking for distraction.

"I asked. He said he'd grab some while we're at the shop. And that he doesn't need much."

"Wish I could say that," she muttered as she gathered eggs and bread for toast.

"You get used to it," Jace said.

She glanced at him. Wanted to ask how he'd gotten used to it, but after the story about Max she hesitated to dig into his life anymore. And instead, because he was looking at the eggs and bread rather more raptly than they deserved, she asked if he was hungry.

"Maybe a little. But I was just thinking about that french toast your mom used to make."

She smiled warmly. "It was the best, wasn't it?"

"I always tried to guess what days she would make it and come over early those days, before Cory and I left for school, hoping she'd make extra for me. I couldn't believe how often I guessed right."

"Silly boy. She made it *because* you came over early and she knew you loved it."

He stared at her. "She did?"

"More than once she put what she'd planned to make away and got out the bread and eggs and spices while Cory went to open the door. Used to tick Cory off—he didn't like it as much as you did."

He looked stunned. Such a simple thing, and he looked stunned. Was it so very unusual to him that somebody would care enough to pay attention to what he liked? That someone would do what her mother had? For him?

She was beginning to realize that even though she'd known his father was harsh and cold, even cruel, she hadn't had the slightest idea what his life had really been like. Which made it all the more amazing that he'd turned out to be the guy she could count on, who would come over a thousand miles to help, just because he'd made a promise years ago.

And she had a thought that was both alluring and frightening: she found the Jace of today even more tempting.

Chapter 7

"I thought you were fixing eggs and bacon," Jace said as she put away the bacon and got out bread.

"I changed my mind," Cassie said.

I thought we were having eggs, not french toast again.
I changed my mind.

He'd heard the exchange between Cory and Mrs. Grant more than once and had naively believed it was that simple. That Cassie's mother had done that just for him felt oddly overwhelming.

A cold nose nudged his fingers. He looked startled; he hadn't even heard Cutter get up. Instinctively Jace scratched that spot he'd discovered he liked, and the animal leaned into him. And as before he felt oddly calmed, as if some of the dog's own serenity had seeped into him through the contact.

"It'll be good," Cassie said. "Mom taught me."

She said it easily enough as she worked, with only a tinge of sadness beneath the light words, so he didn't offer any apology for making her think of the absence of that loving presence.

"I never doubted it," he said. "I feel guilty making you cook, though."

"I would have fixed breakfast anyway." She glanced toward the clock, which was within two minutes of flashing over to six. "Not like I don't have time this morning," she added.

"You didn't have to get up this early."

She gave an inelegant snort. "Right. So I should just sleep in while the menfolk look out for me, is that it?"

"I just meant you don't have to disrupt your schedule. Unless…did I wake you? I tried to be quiet, but there's a—"

"Board. I know. It and I are old adversaries." She grinned then. "Sometimes I think my dad left it that way on purpose. So he'd always know if I left my room at night."

"Ouch. How many times did you get in trouble?"

"It took me until I was about fifteen to realize there was a pattern. But I finally realized that if I snuck out of my room at night and went to play a video game or watch TV, he let me get away with it. But if I took one step toward the front or back door, I was—" she gestured at the bread slices she'd just dropped in a skillet "—toast."

Jace's brow furrowed. "Why would he let you get away with it as long as you stayed in the house?"

"I asked him once I figured it out. He said he let me get away with the harmless stuff because every kid needed to test the limits. And he figured once I realized how tired I was at school the next day, I'd eventually decide it wasn't worth it." She smiled. "I did."

"Your dad was a smart guy."

"My dad loved me," she said simply. And then she looked at him, her eyes more green than gold this morning. "And believe me, Jace, I know just how lucky I was."

"Don't."

His voice was sharper than he'd meant it to be, but after what he'd let out about Max—and he still didn't know why, he never talked about the way his father had been—he knew she was probably feeling sorry for him. And pity was the last thing he wanted. Especially from her.

"Don't what? Acknowledge how lucky I was to have the parents I had?" He felt a bit abashed; he hadn't thought of it like that. He'd been too focused on the difference between hers and his. But then she added quietly, "Or don't remind you that you weren't so lucky? I'm guessing you don't need me to do that."

No. He didn't. But he felt compelled to differentiate. "My mom's okay. She did what she could. And now she's better than okay."

"I'm glad she's doing well."

"It was a long haul, but we made it."

"A long haul?"

He grimaced. He didn't want to talk about it. Couldn't take any more of that pity, or even sympathy. Not from her.

"Doesn't matter anymore," he said with finality.

She let it go. At least she wasn't a prodder, he thought, using his term for the kind of woman who couldn't rest until she got your whole miserable life story out of you.

The french toast was as good as he remembered, and he said so. Cassie smiled, clearly genuinely pleased. They cleared up, and Cassie decided there was no use just killing time, so she might as well head to the shop. Jace didn't argue the point, since killing time would likely mean talking. It was only the natural thing that old friends who hadn't seen each other in a long time would do, but he'd already blabbed enough. Besides, they weren't exactly old friends.

He just wasn't sure what they were. Or how to stop the crazy feelings this all grown-up Cassie raised in him.

"Did you leave your car at the Foxworth place?" Cassidy asked as they walked out to the driveway—the house had never had a garage, only the carport, hence the shed her father had built in the back to store his tools—and got in her little SUV to head to the flower shop. She was opening today, she'd told him, and would be handling it all until May Martinez, her best employee and biggest help, got there at noon. Cutter had been on her heels all the way to the car, obviously intending to go with them, so she'd let him in the back first. She wondered what the poor dog thought of being left with strangers. It certainly didn't seem to bother him. And she'd already seen that the animal knew his own mind. He couldn't have made it any clearer that he was sticking with them.

There was a pause before Jace muttered, "Car's at home."

He sounded…not angry, not even upset, just on edge. Or grumpy. Something.

Odd, she thought as he lapsed into silence again. It never used to be like pulling teeth to get him to talk. "So what are you doing with yourself these days? Who do I need to thank for giving you time off?"

"Want a list?" he asked, sounding a bit sour again.

"Is there one?" she countered. She didn't have as much patience as usual since this had begun. And even less, it seemed, since Jace had arrived. She tried to dig some up. "I just wondered what big architectural firm you landed with."

"None."

"But I thought—"

"I gave up on that idea years ago."

He said it so brittlely she didn't dare push. They were at the shop anyway, so she focused on pulling into her regular spot in the three-car space in back with much more concentration than the familiar task required.

She stayed silent until she opened the back door into the storeroom, but then a gasp of shock escaped her. Rafe Crawford was sitting at the big arranging table, typing something on the keyboard of a rather industrial-looking laptop that sat next to an open backpack.

Instinctively she looked at her key ring, certain the door had been locked. Without looking up, Rafe said, "It was locked. And I relocked it after I got in."

She watched Cutter walk over and greet the man who'd abandoned him to strangers. Or put him to work, she wasn't sure which. "And I suppose I shouldn't ask how?"

Rafe gave her that half shrug she guessed must be a habit, given how often she'd already seen it. Men and their shrugging, she thought. "It's not a bad lock, but I'd put a dead bolt back there if I were you."

"I'll do that," Jace said.

"Good," Rafe said. "Why don't you go get one now? Hardware store down the street. I've got things to finish here." If Jace was startled, it didn't show. Still without looking up, Rafe reached into his pocket and pulled out a few bills, slid the top one off with his thumb and handed it to Jace. "That should do it."

"Wait," she protested, "if it's for the shop I should—"

"It's for this case, so Foxworth will cover it."

Jace crumpled the fifty and shoved it into a front pocket. Without another word he turned on his heel and walked back out the way they'd come in. Cassidy stared after him, wondering what had stung him this time.

The bag with the dead bolt assembly swung as he walked. He'd been grateful no one he knew was in the hardware store, so the transaction had been quick and painless. As he was leaving he spotted, of all people, Mr. Gresham, his former geometry teacher, heading toward him. Of all the people he didn't want to see in this town, he was near the top of the list.

You've got a knack, Jace, for three-dimensional thinking. And you can draw. You should consider architecture.

An odd sort of panic seized him, and he dodged through the nearest doorway. Mr. Gresham—he looked older, obviously, but still had that energetic stride— never even glanced his way, his gaze intent on an apparent list in his hand.

Crazy. That's how crazy his life was, that the person he wanted to see least was the man who'd encouraged him most. Nearly the only one who had encouraged him; most of the rest had been too exasperated at the way his mind worked. He remembered all the times in other classes that he got to the right answer but in a very different way than the teacher had explained it. Only Mr. Gresham had taken the time to have him explain the way he'd done it, had made him prove that method would work with other parameters, had ended up pronouncing it valid for Jace himself and given him full credit for the answer.

The others had marked him down for not following the proper methodology, as they put it.

"Your turn, buddy," a slightly impatient voice said from behind him. Only then did he realize he'd dodged into the local coffee provider and the woman behind the counter was waiting.

"Uh…yeah. Sorry."

He turned toward the front, hastily ordered a plain black coffee, paid for it with the change from the dead bolt, and walked out hoping Rafe didn't mind. Especially since it was for him; another shot of caffeine and he himself would be climbing the walls, a situation he was already too close to.

Cassie had opened the shop while he was gone, but she was on the phone now, apparently with a supplier. Cutter was at her feet but got up and came to greet him as he stepped into the back room through the door Rafe opened. He gave the dog a pat, then set the coffee on the table within Rafe's reach. That got him a sideways look.

"No double-wide frosted mocha frappé latte with a shot and a whipped cream chaser? I'm hurt."

It took Jace a second to be sure he was joking. "I don't even know what that…whatever you said is."

"Since I just made it up, nonexistent," Rafe said with a wry expression. "Thanks."

Jace smiled then. He glanced over at Cassie, who was making notes on the computer in the corner of the room.

"She's efficient," Rafe said.

"Always was."

Rafe studied him for a moment, but Jace couldn't read his expression. He got the feeling no one could if he didn't want them to. Except maybe that dog.

"We need to talk about the plan for this location."

Jace blinked. "I figured it was just I stick to her like glue."

"Yes. You go where she goes. But also keep an eye outside, like you did when you heard the noise. Photos, if you can get them, of anybody hanging around."

"Photos?" Belatedly he realized. "Oh. The phone."

Rafe nodded and thankfully didn't ask why that hadn't been his first thought, as it would be with most these days. Instead he just continued. "If you can do it without them catching on, fine, but if it's a choice between letting them get too close and getting a good image, err on the side of caution."

"Absolutely." There was no doubt in his mind Cassie's safety was the first priority, despite her quick "Catch him" assessment.

"There's a chance, if he's curious about you, he might actually come in. So act like an infatuated boyfriend."

He grimaced. "Not sure I know how." *But I could learn. With Cassie.*

At the thought of that kind of lesson, heat kicked through him. He tried to quash it, but it seemed to have taken up residence from the moment she'd opened her front door and he'd seen not the awkward kid he remembered, but a luscious, tempting woman.

"I could give you lessons," Rafe said drily, "since it's all around me these days. Thanks to this clown," he added with a glance and a nod toward Cutter.

Jace blinked. "Him? Why?"

"Didn't I mention that this hardworking dog works the hardest at playing matchmaker?"

Jace laughed then. Rafe only looked rather glum. Then he gave one of those half shrugs that seemed to say, "You'll find out." The only thing he actually said was, "If you can get even a distant photo, our tech guy can work miracles."

"Okay."

Cassie had hung up finally, but just as she turned to them, the bell rang out front, indicating someone had come in, and she reversed course. Jace instantly moved to where he could see the customer and relaxed when he saw a young woman holding a baby at the counter. He started to turn to go back, but just then Cassie walked around and reached out to run the back of her fingers over the baby's cheek. The mother laughed, and the next thing he knew she'd handed the baby over to Cassie, who took it—he had no idea what sex it was—and cradled it in her arms.

He only had time to wonder if that was something that was just instinctive in women, knowing how to hold a baby, before the oddest sensation seized him. The rightness of it, or something. Cassie should have babies. She would be good for them and to them. It took him a moment to realize what he was feeling was envy. For the lucky guy sometime in the future who would father those babies. Even for the babies, who would have loving parents, just as she'd had.

He turned away sharply, wondering what was wrong with him. Having a hot, purely sexual reaction to a beautiful woman he understood, but what the hell was this about?

For distraction he walked over to inspect the back door, which was thankfully made of wood, then went in search of tools to put in the dead bolt. He'd installed one twice before, in the less than friendly neighborhoods he and his mother had lived in before now. Cassie had the basics here but no more; what he was going to need was a power drill motor with a good-size bit.

"Don't suppose you have power tools in that trunk full of goodies?" he asked Rafe.

"Depends on your definition of power tools," the man answered levelly.

He could only imagine. He turned and walked back. "I'm sure Cassie still has some of her dad's. I'll ask her." Rafe nodded, still intent on the screen before him. "What's that?"

"Called a friend of ours with the sheriff's office. Ran checks on her employees, nothing popped. Same on customers and friends, except for one who's got a leaning toward a few drinks too many and one who can't keep her foot off the accelerator."

"Jessica Goodman, I'll bet," he said instantly. "For her speed limits were more like guidelines."

Rafe's mouth quirked as he nodded to confirm Jace's guess.

"I can't think of anybody she's connected to who would do this. I mean it's weird, the guy just hanging around, never approaching, just watching. For what?"

"That is a very good question," Rafe said. "Think about it."

Jace frowned slightly. He'd been doing nothing else. But he simply couldn't imagine anyone wanting to hurt Cassie. She was the proverbial girl next door, sweet, kind, generous.

Of course she's also blossomed into a beautiful woman. And there are a lot of guys out there who would want to go after that.

And he hated them all with a fierceness that shocked him.

"You should have come out and said hello."

He spun around as Cassie came back, speaking cheerfully. "What?"

"Brittany would have loved to have seen you."

He stared at her. Brittany? "That was... Brittany Cross?"

"Well, Rios now," Cassie said. "Now don't tell me you didn't recognize her. She had the biggest crush on you junior year."

He hadn't. She'd been blonde then. "She did?"

Cassie laughed. "That was half of what was so charming about you. You never realized any of us were crushing on you."

He'd had about enough of feeling totally disconcerted. "I knew you were," he said bluntly.

If he'd meant to embarrass her—and he wasn't sure he had—he failed. She just waved a hand airily. "Only after Cory told you."

"Well…yeah." He scrambled for something else, anything else to talk about other than the fact that Cassidy Grant had once thought he hung the moon. "Wait…you said Rios. You don't mean she married Rick Rios?"

"Yep."

"But she hated him," Jace said; more than once Brittany had tossed out insults about the rich guy who had transferred in and thought he was the big man on campus.

"I think that was cover for how she really felt."

"But—"

"Can you two can forgo the nostalgia for a minute and come take a look at this?"

Rafe sounded merely amused, but Jace wondered if underneath he was wearying of having to listen to them.

You have history.

He'd been right about that. What they didn't have was a future. At least not together. No, Cassie would settle down with someone steady, solid, who could handle a normal job without going crazy. She would have those kids and a happy life. And she deserved it. She may have been through a different kind of hell than he had, but it had been hell nevertheless.

Belatedly he realized she had gone to do as Rafe had asked. She was looking over his shoulder at the laptop he'd been working on, and when he got there, he recognized a view of the area outside the front of the shop.

"You've been busy," he said, realizing the man must have installed a security camera out front.

"And I appreciate it," Cassie said. "I just hope it isn't off-putting to customers."

"Likely they'll never notice. It's about the size of a golf ball, and it's up under the eave of the building."

"And you just happen to have that stuff with you?" Jace asked.

"We keep a few helpful things handy," Rafe said.

"She needs one of these at the house. And lights on a motion sensor."

Rafe flicked him a sideways glance with a nod. "You can handle the lights. Camera's already installed. It'll connect with your phones. I'll show you later."

"When," Cassie asked, clearly startled, "did you do that?"

"Last night."

"I didn't hear a thing," Cassie said, looking half concerned, half impressed. Jace was all impressed.

Rafe only shrugged and moved on. "What I wanted you to look at is this." He hit a couple of keys, and the image on the screen ran rapidly backward for a few seconds. He hit another key, and it froze. The time stamp in the lower corner said 5:00 a.m., long before they'd arrived, and long before sunrise.

Jace heard Cassie's breath catch as she stared at the image.

"Him?" Rafe asked.

Jace leaned closer to look at the figure clad in a dark jacket, the hood pulled up to shadow his face.

"It…he looks the same. Dressed the same. Same height, build."

"Same body language?"

She frowned. "No. He's usually more…wary. Looking around, I mean."

Rafe nodded. "He's feeling safe here, because it's dark, and no one's here to spot him."

"But why here, in the middle of the night? When I'm at home? Did he…do something here, to the shop?" She looked around with concern.

"Maybe plant a camera of his own?" Jace asked.

"Good questions all," Rafe said. "But there's another this raises."

"Which is?" Cassie asked.

"That maybe he's waiting for something. Or someone." He looked at Cassie. "He hasn't come at you, made a move even though you've been here in the open, and home alone. Now he may just be working himself up to it, but…"

She looked puzzled. "But?"

"So," Jace said, feeling a spurt of relief as he realized what Rafe had meant earlier, "maybe it's not really you he's after."

Chapter 8

Cassie stared at Rafe, then shifted her gaze back to the man in the image on the laptop screen, that shadowy shape. The man who had been stalking…maybe not her?

Instead of relieved, as Jace was feeling, she looked only puzzled. "What on earth could he be looking or waiting for? This is a flower shop—it's not like we have huge amounts of money coming through here."

"What about something else?" Jace asked. "I mean deliveries, that could be a cover for something, couldn't it?"

"Could be," Rafe said neutrally.

"I do most of the arrangements," Cassie said. "And May does the rest. But there's no way she would be involved in anything…illicit."

"Maybe not knowingly," Jace said.

"We still don't have enough volume to be useful for anything in bulk," she said.

Jace shifted on his feet beside her as he straightened from looking at the screen. He realized his jaw was tight and tried to relax it.

"What?" she asked him.

"Just thinking. Some things don't need volume to be profitable."

She stared at him, her brow furrowed with disbelief. "What? You think we're smuggling drugs in with the chrysanthemums? How? In the little preservative packets, maybe?"

"Cassie," he began, but she was rolling now.

"Or maybe diamonds? That's big money, small volume, right? Maybe in among those little glass pebbles we sometimes put in the bottom of the vases? Maybe—"

"Cassie, stop. I wasn't accusing." His mouth quirked upward. "Although I gotta say, those are pretty good ideas, and we'd be in trouble if you ever decided to turn bad on the world."

He got a smile out of her before Rafe cleared his throat and said, "And if I was my boss, I'd have a tactful way to say we need to focus here."

"Oh. Yeah," Jace said.

"Sorry," Cassie added.

The shop phone rang. Cassie glanced at the caller ID and sighed. "Tiffany, probably changing her choices for the wedding again. This time she'll probably want orchids for a Christmas wedding."

He remembered the name. "She and Brady finally tying the knot?" he asked as she started across the room to the phone. The couple had been inseparable through all of high school. He would have figured they'd have gotten married the minute they graduated.

She stopped in her tracks. Her gaze shot back to his face. "Brady is dead. Years ago. Afghanistan."

Jace expelled a harsh breath. "Damn."

"Yes," Cassie said grimly, letting the phone ring a second time.

Jace noticed Rafe had gone very still. "Is she all right?" he asked. "And his family, are they?"

Jace had the strangest feeling that if Cassie answered no, they weren't, this man would do something about it.

"She'll never be whole again," Cassie said frankly on the third ring, "but her fiancé knows that. He was Brady's best friend. I don't know what kind of marriage they'll have, but I do know they will both give it their best. And Brady's parents know it, too. They're as accepting as they can be, under the circumstances."

Cassie grabbed up the phone and answered in a cheerful tone. Jace shook off the shiver that ran through him and turned back to Rafe.

"If he's not—thank goodness—after her, then who? Or what?" he asked.

Rafe stood up, stretching. He started to walk around the back room, and Jace saw the slight limp he'd noticed before was a bit more pronounced now, although it didn't hinder his movement much. He seemed to be pushing that leg harder, flexing it more. After three circuits his gait was back to what Jace guessed was normal for him, the hitch barely noticeable unless you knew to look.

"If I knew that," Rafe said finally, "this would be over and you could go home."

Go home. Back to the grind his life there had become? He'd done what he'd set out to do there, and that gave him a great deal of satisfaction, but he didn't think he could stomach going back to that same life.

"Not happy about that idea, are you?" Rafe asked.

Jace didn't bother trying to deny it. Somehow he guessed lying to this man would be a very sizable mistake. "No. I did what I needed to do there."

"So the world's wide-open."

He gave a rueful snort. "Hardly."

"You're young, smart, healthy," Rafe said.

"And broke, minus a college education, and I also think weird. I always have."

Rafe seemed to consider this for a moment. "Weird how?"

Jace shrugged. Tamped down all the memories, the yelling, the pure hatred his father had expressed for everything about him, but especially the way he thought. "I can figure things out, but I don't take the approved route." His mouth twisted. "I got in trouble in elementary school countless times because I answered word questions with pictures, or drew math problems instead of just working them out. And even those I did weird."

"How?"

He shrugged again. He rarely revisited these days, but this guy was helping them, so he didn't feel like he could shut this down. "Seven apples minus three airplanes. They used to insist I had to at least use all apples. I thought it was the numbers that mattered."

"But you got to the right place?"

"Usually."

"Just not the way they thought you should?" Rafe asked, not clarifying who he meant by "they," which told Jace he understood.

"Exactly."

"Don't join the military then," Rafe said, his tone wry.

"I figured." He nodded toward where Cassie was on the phone, listening intently. "Besides, I wouldn't want my mom to ever get the kind of news Brady's did. I'm all she's got left."

"Yet when Cassidy called, you left her and came."

He met the other man's eyes then. "I told you. I made a promise. And my mother was the first one to say I had to keep it."

He didn't say anything more, but he had the oddest feeling this man was hearing much more than he'd said. He supposed you didn't get that kind of look in your eyes without learning a lot of life's lessons the hard way.

"She changed her mind again?" he asked when Cassie hung up and came back.

"And then unchanged it. Again."

"You're very patient."

"After what she's been through, it's the least I can do. I'm just glad she's found someone who will love her and give her the best life he can."

"Even knowing she might never love him the way she did Brady?"

"I think for Neil, it will be enough that she'll let him love her."

He had never in his life been that crazy about somebody. Not that he'd gone looking—he'd never had time.

And now here you are, with a woman who's already driving you crazy, and no amount of remembering the kid she once was is helping.

He gave himself an inward shake. He'd come here because Cassie was being stalked. And now it appeared there was more to it than he'd first thought. Yet still his mind kept veering back to those things he'd never had time for. It seemed all he'd heard about since he'd gotten here was people who'd died, people getting married, people together or not, and it was making him edgy.

"I realized on my way to the hardware store that this area has changed in ten years," he said abruptly. "I think I should walk around a bit, get familiar. Just in case."

Rafe looked at him. "Not a bad idea. Take Cutter. He can be your excuse." He gave a slight cough as he reached into a side pocket of the backpack and pulled out a leather leash, which he handed to Jace. "He's got good leash manners, so if he goes weird on you, it'll be because something's up you should pay attention to. If he does, come back or call me, whichever is quickest."

"You mean the guy?"

"He'll let you know." Rafe looked at him consideringly. "And help, if you get into trouble."

Cassie made a small sound. "Maybe you shouldn't—"

"Why I'm here," he pointed out to her, more sharply than he'd meant to.

"He'll be fine," Rafe said. He nodded at Jace. "I've seen his win list."

Cassie reacted again, but this time it was with a chagrin that was gratifying. "I forgot. Just how good you are."

"Were," he said. Then, to Rafe, he admitted with a grimace, "Haven't had much chance to practice for a long time."

"Cutter'll help you hold him off so you can call, if necessary," Rafe said mildly.

After a moment Jace just nodded. But he was churning a bit inside; he'd gone into martial arts to feel stronger, to gain the confidence to stand up to his father. And he had been good at it, but he'd never used it in a real-life situation.

He became aware of a warm pressure on his leg and looked down to see Cutter leaning against him. This time it made sense at least; he had the leash in his hand. He took advantage of that fact to bend down and fasten it to the dog's collar. And the moment he brushed a hand over the dog's head he felt better, steadier.

But he still wasn't steady enough to meet Cassie's gaze, and left without looking at her.

Cassie watched as Jace turned his back and walked out with the dog. "I used to worry about him. I didn't think I still would."

Rafe looked at her. "Worry?"

"I didn't understand, as a kid, except that his father was mean. Then later I heard him once, screaming at Jace, calling him awful names, telling him he was useless, a burden, and that he wished he'd never been born."

She felt a shiver go through her; she would never, ever forget the look of shame and humiliation on Jace's young face when he realized she was there and had heard.

"I wish we could have done…" She stopped. The futility of wishing was something she'd learned well after her parents died.

"From a couple of things he said, I think your family did. You were a…refuge for him."

"Not enough," she said, rather fiercely.

"Sometimes all you need is a little, to hang on." His voice was a little scratchy again, and she seized on that as distraction and went to the sink in the corner and got him a glass of water.

"Are you getting sick?" she asked as she handed it to him. To her surprise he chuckled.

"No. I just don't usually talk this much. My throat's not used to it."

"I... Thank you for believing me."

He gestured at the laptop. "If I hadn't, him showing up here in the dark would have convinced me."

While she was now hopeful, at least, that she personally wasn't the man's target, she still had absolutely no idea what he could be after if it wasn't her. But before she could dwell on it, the door chime rang again. She glanced out, saw Mrs. Snider, who was organizing a fund-raising auction for the local animal shelter. The shop was donating a few flower arrangements for the event. They couldn't afford anything more, but she wanted to do what she could.

By the time they were done and Mrs. Snider had gone, Jace and Cutter were back, reporting that nothing eventful had happened on their walk. And he seemed to have regained his calm after those rough moments when Rafe had guessed accurately at his painful history.

"I was thinking, though," Jace said as he unclipped the leash and handed it back to Rafe. "If this guy is after something, not someone, then obviously he doesn't know where it is. But if he thinks Cassie does, that could be as bad as if he was after her in the first place."

That easily, her hopeful relief vanished. She should have thought of that herself, but instead she'd just been glad there could be another reason for the stranger's presence.

"But…there's nothing. I don't know anything, or about anything worth this."

"Then it's something you don't know about, or don't realize what it's worth," Jace said.

She frowned as she looked at him. "Something like what? And why would I have it or know about it?" She let out a frustrated sound. "This doesn't make any sense."

Jace didn't answer but looked thoughtful, as if something had occurred to him. And Rafe was watching Jace.

But before she could ask what he was thinking, the bell in front rang yet again. Normally she'd be happy about any customer walking in, but at this moment it was a distraction. She would be glad when May got here to take over, but in the meantime she put on her welcoming smile and walked out into the shop.

"I'd like to say something."

Jace looked up at Cassidy from the square white box of takeout sweet-and-sour chicken he was working on. It had been a long day and they were still here, although she'd closed up. Once May had arrived to take over the front of the shop, Cassidy had enough online orders to deal with that there had been little time to talk after Rafe had packed up his gear—but not Cutter—and left to do…whatever it was he was going to do. She hoped that included some sleep, since apparently he'd been up since they'd arrived yesterday. It was late, dark, and she was ready to go home, but there was something she wanted to say first.

"What?" Jace asked, sounding wary.

"I know you don't want sympathy—" he tensed, but she kept going "—and it's not that, not really. I just want to say that I wish we'd done more back then, anything to help you."

"You did." His voice was as tight as that muscle in his jaw. "Your family, your folks, were sometimes the only way I hung on. You did plenty."

"Not enough. We should have—"

"Your dad wanted to." It sounded as if he wished he hadn't said it even as the words came out.

She blinked. "What?"

"He talked to me about it once. He asked me if…my father hit me, or my mom."

She sucked in a breath as he voiced what she had feared, all those years ago. "Did he ever?" she asked, feeling a little fierce.

"No." He grimaced. "He never had to. He was so much bigger than her, and me until my junior year, that his rage, all his yelling and hitting other things was enough."

"That wasn't just yelling, Jace. That was verbal abuse."

Jace grimaced again. "He just…hated me. Your dad said once he'd talk to him, confront him. I asked him— hell, I begged him not to. Because it would only make things worse. That he probably would start hitting me then."

She was a little bit stunned. "My dad never told me that. But I should have known. They could never witness what was happening to you and not at least try to help. It's who they were."

He met her gaze then, and this time it was she who felt the rush of sympathy. "They were good people, Cassie. The best."

"Yes." Tears stung her eyes, the sudden upsurge of grief, even after all this time, catching her off guard.

Cutter moved then, oddly getting to his feet and nudging at Jace, who set down the box of food. And then he moved as well, quickly, his arms enveloping her in a rather fierce hug. She let him, for at this moment she needed it too badly to say no.

"I'm sorry," she said, fighting the tears, finding the will to do it as if he were lending it to her. She clung to him, to his warmth and solid strength. "It probably seems silly after all this time—"

"Don't. Grief is…it's like water behind a dam. It holds most of the time, but if the pressure builds too much it will leak, or even overflow, sometimes when and where you least expect it."

He spoke with flat, utter knowledge. And for the first time she realized he had, if not people, things to grieve. Like having the most basic, fundamental kind of trust betrayed. "Jace," she began.

"I grieved them, too, Cassie," he said softly. "They were the only reason I ever knew my father's way was wrong."

She shivered then slipped her arms around him. And suddenly the comfort was going both ways.

They stood there for a long time. Until gradually, slowly, the warmth shifted, changed somehow. And the memories of how much she had once wanted this, to be held in Jace's arms, nearly swamped her. She didn't want to move, didn't want it to end, but she was careening dangerously close to doing something stupid. Like trying to kiss him.

Look at him. You'll see that friend-zone look, that expression that will remind you he's just comforting his best friend's little sister.

She tilted her head back to do just that. And instead of that warm, friendly Jace look, she saw something much hotter kindling in the depths of those blue eyes she'd always loved. His head lowered, and she saw his lips part. Lower still and she could feel the heat of him, could hear that his breathing had gotten a little ragged, just as her own had quickened.

She felt the urge to close her eyes but didn't. Jace, her Jace, was going to kiss her, and she wanted to see and remember every second of it. And so she saw the moment when his eyes widened slightly. The moment when his breath stopped for an instant. She held her own, as if even breathing could shatter this precious moment in time.

And then he was kissing her, but not as she'd expected. Instead of those lips on hers, they were brushing away the last of her tears, kissing them away in a way that was warm, tender and utterly unsexual.

Disappointment flooded through her.

"Okay now?" he asked, as if he wanted to back away but wouldn't if she still needed comforting. But comfort had been the last thing on her mind in those seconds.

"Fine. Thank you," she said stiffly, and disappointment was replaced by embarrassment as she pulled out of his arms.

He jammed his hands into his front pockets and backed up a long step. As if he couldn't wait to get clear of her. And he looked as if he'd had a very narrow escape. The embarrassment blossomed until she was very afraid it must be obvious to him.

What was obvious to her was that she had somehow regressed into adolescence, and she'd be lucky if she didn't scare him off with that silliness.

Chapter 9

Jace searched for anything to feign interest in, anything to keep from looking at Cassie again, to keep from thinking about what he'd almost done. He stopped before a tub full of red flowers. Carnations. Maybe. Whatever they were, they gave him something to dwell on for a moment. They couldn't be local, not this time of year; he'd picked up a bit by osmosis back in the days he'd spent at the Grant house. Then again, what did he know, for sure?

Well, except that he'd almost laid the lip lock to end all lip locks on Cory's little sister. That had to violate the bro code a couple of different ways. Except…she wasn't that little sister anymore. No, Cassidy Grant was all woman now, with those changeable eyes and that long, silky fall of hair and…curves. Luscious, finger-curling curves. His mother had always said she would blossom someday. He'd thought she was just making a pun on the family flower business, but now he knew what she'd meant.

He didn't know how long he'd been standing there staring at those red flowers, but he gathered it had been a bit too long when she said, rather pointedly, "They're just carnations. Shipped in from California."

He remembered suddenly the large commercial flower fields he'd often seen alongside the interstate. He felt stupid—he'd never really thought about them getting shipped as far away as here. Not that that had stopped him from thinking about the Grants, wondering how they were.

And then that day had come when for the first time in a very long time Cory had called him and not wanted money. It was the most shaken he'd ever heard his friend, and when he told him what had happened Jace was so shaken himself he'd nearly collapsed on the floor of the tiny apartment they were in by then.

"Jace?"

He turned then. "Sorry," he muttered. "Just…thinking."

He didn't want to say about what, for fear she'd start crying again, and this time he wouldn't be able to stop with just comforting.

It's Cassie—get a grip. Just because you've been living like a monk for way too long doesn't mean you jump the first woman you're close to. Especially when it's Cory's sister. The girl you've known most of your life.

It didn't help. Because when he looked at her now, he didn't see Cory's little sister anymore. He saw the lovely, amazing woman she'd become.

"Don't hurt yourself," she said.

He frowned, then realized she was responding to his "just thinking" comment. Like she used to, to both him and her brother, all those years ago.

"Too late," he responded, almost automatically. Just as he used to.

She smiled then, and it was the old, sweet Cassie looking at him and he could breathe normally again. Maybe she hadn't noticed, hadn't realized what he'd almost done.

Maybe.

But for the briefest moment there he'd seen…something. In her eyes, in the way they went all golden, in her mouth, and the way her lips had parted. As if she not only knew what he was about to do but wanted it.

Wanted it. Him.

He clamped down on the sudden rush of heat that poured through him. And clung to the explanation that it had just been too damned long.

"Did I ever really thank you for coming?" she asked.

"Yeah. You did."

"I meant it. Not everyone would drop what they were doing to come all this way for a friend's sister."

"I promised."

"I know." Her mouth twisted slightly. "Something else not everyone does. Keep promises."

"That's why some of us do."

She studied him silently for a moment. Long enough that he started to feel restless. Then, softly, she said, "Your father certainly didn't."

He blinked. Took a half step back. Felt the carnations brush against his back.

"I won't be like him. Ever."

It broke from him under his breath, but he knew she heard it. He couldn't seem to stop it. Maybe it was being here, back in this town where he'd spent those painful years, trying so hard not to put a foot wrong, never realizing that there was no way he could put a foot right.

"Of course you won't." She said it confidently, as if she were as certain as she was that the sun would rise tomorrow.

He wanted to hug her again. To just hold her. But that was all he'd intended the first time, and then he'd let it turn into something else, something very different. He'd—

A low growl from Cutter cut through his thoughts. The dog was on his feet, head turned toward the back door. The change in the animal was instant and obvious; he was no longer the relaxed companion, seemingly happy to just be lolling around with them. This was the guard Rafe had promised he would be.

"Maybe it's just somebody walking down the alley," Cassie said.

"Maybe," Jace said, watching the dog. "Can you call up the camera feed?"

"Oh," she said, clearly not yet used to the extra security they'd set up. "Of course."

She went quickly to the computer in the corner, where Rafe had directed the feed from the cameras he'd installed. The screen came up, split top and bottom, top showing the front of the shop, where the only things moving were cars passing on the street, the bottom showing the darker alley, just outside that door. He couldn't see anything or anyone moving, but there were shadowy places outside the camera's field.

And Cutter was still growling.

"You need a brighter light out there," he muttered.

He looked toward the door. Cutter's head was down, his ears flattened. The growl became deeper, more insistent. And then the dog looked back over his shoulder at him. The "Come on!" couldn't have been clearer. Automatically Jace started toward him.

"Picture, remember?"

He heard the concern in her voice, wasn't sure if what he was feeling was gratification at the worry, or insult at the hint that he shouldn't do anything more than snap a photo of the guy, if indeed that's who it was. He was inclined to think so; Rafe had been utterly confident the dog would signal, and it certainly seemed he was.

"Yeah," he muttered, but he did pull the phone out of his pocket and call up the camera app. He thought for a brief moment and switched it to video.

Cutter was quiet, and Jace wondered if it was because he knew his message had been received and understood. This was an entirely different beast than sweet but dopey Max. He smothered the jab of pain; he was used to it, since it happened every time he thought of the loving, innocent dog who had tried to stand between him and the towering rage of the man who had been his father, if only biologically.

He reached for the door handle. Cutter was practically dancing with eagerness now, to get out and likely at whatever he'd heard or scented. He yanked the door open quickly. The dog bolted out. Jace heard a scrabbling in the shadows near the dumpster. Saw the shape. Started the camera, but followed the dog.

They went past Cassie's car, which announced her

presence inside, and Jace felt a stab of concern; would the guy have broken in, knowing she was there? Was he getting bolder? Or more desperate?

Cutter unexpectedly dodged right around the dumpster, snarling now. His change in direction apparently startled the man in the shadows—Jace could see it was a man now—and he stumbled back three steps. And into the light from the back of the Chinese restaurant next door. Jace froze, holding the camera steady as the man was lit up for a full second. Then he was running, Cutter spinning back around and going after him.

Jace had the crazy thought that the dog had intentionally diverted to push the guy into the light but dismissed it. He shoved the phone back in his pocket and went after them both, but the man made it to a dark-colored sedan parked a few strides away. He'd left the engine running and was inside in an instant.

And in that instant headlights came on, illuminating Cutter. Jace realized the dog would have had him if not for that little diversion, and again he wondered. But then the man slammed the car into gear and hit the accelerator.

Jace froze. The car revving, the dog barking—it all collided in his head against the freshly recalled memory of Max.

"No!" he yelled and ran for the dog. Not again, not again, not again...

Cutter looked back at his shout. For an instant the dog seemed as frozen as he had been. And then, suddenly, unexpectedly, the animal abandoned the pursuit that had been his only focus. He spun around and raced back toward Jace. He reached him and rose up on his hind legs, his front paws pushing against his chest. Lightly, but definitely, demanding Jace look at him. He did, even as he heard the car pulling away.

Jace sagged against the back wall of the restaurant as Cutter leaned into him. He threw his arms around the dog, and Cutter nudged him and licked his face. It was an oddly soothing touch, and his hammering heart began to calm.

But that voice in his head did not.

You're a lot of help. Guy could have killed her, with you standing there immobilized by a stupid memory. Even Cutter had to give up the chase to come back and shake you out of it. Useless. Worthless.

Cutter barked, sharply, in a "snap out of it!" kind of tone. It cut off the old litany he hadn't fallen prey to in a long time.

Coming back here had been a big mistake. In more ways than one.

Cassidy had been terrified at first, as the seconds ticked past with Jace and the dog still outside in the dark. And she'd heard that car race off.

But she wasn't sure now was much better. After she'd risked opening the door to look, he'd come back. He came in with Cutter sticking to him as if they shared the same skin, and she was nearly as frightened at his expression.

And his monosyllabic answers to the questions she peppered him with.

"Are you all right?"

"Yes."

"Is Cutter?"

"Yes."

"Is he gone?"

"Yes."

"Did you—"

Before she could get that one asked, he pulled out the Foxworth cell phone and set it on the table. "Video," he said.

"Rafe is on the way."

"Good."

There was a bit too much emphasis on that one. "You're sure you're all right? You seem—"

He stopped her with a wave of his hand. And at last said more than one word. "I only want to go through it once."

She could understand that at least. And they didn't have long to wait; Rafe was there less than five minutes after she'd called. Which told her just how fast everything had happened outside.

Rafe looked Jace and Cutter up and down the moment he was inside. The dog went to greet him, plumed tail wagging, but he immediately returned to Jace's side. She saw Rafe watch this, but he didn't speak. He just waited.

"He got away," Jace said flatly.

There was a world of self-condemnation in his voice, and Cassidy frowned. "He had a car, right? I heard it take off."

"Yes."

"You see it?" Rafe asked. Cassidy thought he looked… not puzzled, but as if he realized something was off.

"Not enough." Again that tone. But when Rafe merely waited again, he went on, sounding as if he was having to force every word. "Dark. Four door. Midsize."

"In-state plates?"

"Yes." Jace grimaced. "I only got three numbers."

"But he got video, of the man," Cassidy said, gesturing at the phone Jace had put on the table.

"Only because Cutter got him into the light next door."

One corner of Rafe's mouth lifted at that. He glanced at the dog. "Herded him, did he?"

Jace blinked. "Yeah. Yeah, I guess he did. How did he…?"

"We've surrendered," Rafe said drily. "We don't wonder anymore how he knows what to do and just accept that he does."

She heard Jace take in a deep breath before he went on. "He probably would have had him, too, but I… The car was running, and the guy floored it." He lowered his gaze, shaking his head.

"Let's look at the video," Rafe said, picking up the phone. She'd told him there'd been nothing on the security camera feed, but that Cutter had known someone was out there.

He ran it back on the phone first. At first there was only shadow and noise, whether from Jace's movements or the prowler's, she couldn't tell. And under it all Cutter's deep-throated growling. Then she saw the dark-clad, hooded figure practically careen into the ring of light next door. He recovered quickly and ran toward the car whose dark shape she could barely make out back in the shadows. And then Cutter raced into the frame, headed for the car as well.

The video stopped.

"Useless," Jace muttered.

"Hardly," Rafe said mildly. "I'll send it and the partial plate to Ty—our tech head—and see what he can do. I think there's a moment there, when he looked back, that he might be able to make something of."

Obviously very familiar with the phone, it took him only a moment to send off the video. Then he looked at Jace again.

"Notice anything unexpected, about him or the car?"

Jace shook his head, and again Cassidy got that sense of self-disgust. "He left the car running. And Cutter startled him."

"So he didn't plan on staying long, whether he got in or not," Rafe said.

"Or he wanted a quick getaway," Cassidy said.

Rafe nodded.

"Her car is out there," Jace said flatly. "He had to know she was here."

"But maybe not before," Rafe said. "I noticed when I was outside earlier, the light from back here is hardly visible from out front. And with no windows back here, he could easily not have known until he got back there and saw the car."

"And he knows I'm not alone anymore," Cassidy said, letting every bit of the gratitude for that she was feeling into her voice.

"He knows you have a guard dog, at least," Jace said.

She'd had about enough of that tone in his voice. "And Cutter, too," she said innocently.

A flash of puzzlement crossed his face, then settled into a rather rueful expression. "For somebody who came to help, I didn't do much."

"You did," she retorted, "exactly what you were supposed to do."

"Right she is," Rafe said, opening up the backpack and pulling out his laptop. "You acted exactly as your cover would indicate you would," he said, watching as the computer booted up. He uploaded the video from the phone, put it at full screen and started it. Both she and Jace leaned in to look. Cassidy thought she saw the moment when the man's face was lit, at least in profile, but it went by too fast. Rafe started it again, paused just before the hooded head turned, then moved it forward frame by frame until that instant was frozen in front of them.

She felt a sudden chill. "It's him." Both Jace and Rafe looked at her. "I know, it's not clear, but that nose, and the way he has the hoodie pulled up to cover his mouth…"

Rafe just nodded and went back to run the rest of the video forward in slow motion. Jace slipped an arm around her, as if in reassurance. And that he did it, despite whatever had him so rattled, warmed her as much as the heat from his closeness. Any woman would be lucky to have him.

But she was the one who wanted him. And as she savored the feel of him so close, she realized she meant that in every way it could be taken.

Chapter 10

Jace watched as Rafe put some kibble in the clean flower pot Cassie gave him and set it down for Cutter.

"He'll eat out of it?" she asked.

"Or just about anything. He's used to eating on the run."

Clearly it was true, because the dog went after the food without hesitation. But he didn't, as Jace had expected, empty the makeshift bowl. He left a good handful and then walked over to Jace and sat down. Rafe emptied what was left back into the large, sealable plastic bag he'd brought in and set the bag on the back room table.

"Might as well take that," Rafe said. "Looks like he's staying with you."

"He certainly proved his worth tonight," Cassie said as she leaned down to pet the dark head.

"Unlike some of us," Jace muttered under his breath.

She straightened and looked at him, and for a moment he thought she'd heard what he hadn't meant her to. But she only looked at Rafe. "Have you eaten at all? There's a bit of leftover Chinese here, or you can come back to the house with us and I'll fix something."

"Thank you. I'll take what's here, but I think I should stay clear of your place. Until we find out what this guy is after, I'd like to have a surprise waiting for him."

And you'd definitely be that. Me, I'm just the guy who freaks out over a dog.

"And you two should be very eager to get out of here and go home."

"We should?" Cassie asked, clearly startled. Then it hit her. She glanced at Jace, and he saw faint spots of color in her cheeks.

"Yeah," he said sourly. "We're hot for each other, remember?"

The glance became a stare. And after a painfully silent moment, she said softly, "Yes. I remember."

Jace's breath caught. Heat pooled in him, low and deep. Her eyes were practically glowing, the gold overpowering the green. He stared back at her, unable to think of anything except that moment when he'd wanted to kiss that mouth that even now seemed irresistible.

Rafe gave an audible sigh. "Ten for ten, dog?"

Cassie's expression changed to one of puzzlement as she shifted her gaze to the man doing some kind of search on the laptop. But she, Jace realized, had not heard the man's claim that Cutter was some kind of magical matchmaker. Thankfully.

Rafe didn't look up, only said, "Go ahead. I'll lock up."

"All right," Cassie said, and went to get her jacket from the rack inside the back door. Cutter was on her heels, so Jace picked up the bag of dog food.

They opened the door to the rain that had been hovering all day. Jace, his blood still thinned out by California heat, had never taken off his jacket in the first place. He noticed, unsurprised, that despite the rain Cassie didn't put up the hood on her jacket for the few steps to the car. But then, she'd never been preoccupied with her hair or her looks in general.

Probably because she's always known she's the smartest kid in the room. That's where her pride lies.

He remembered thinking that the day he'd come over after class and they'd found her, as usual, studying. Cory had been teasing her, saying she wouldn't be bad looking if she'd just do something with that stick-straight hair of hers.

"I think that," he'd said, reaching to pull out the pencil she'd used to hold the long strands up in a knot at the back of her head, "is doing something."

She'd jumped, stared at him and blushed as her hair fell back past her shoulders.

Cory had said something that warned Jace he was going to tease her about having a crush on him, and he'd quickly asked, "How does that work, anyway?"

She didn't answer but took the pencil back from him. Silently she gathered up her hair again, twisted it, then rolled it into that knot-looking affair. Then she shoved the pencil through it and let go. It held.

"Amazing," Jace had said lightly, and he'd finally earned a smile.

"You still do that thing with your hair and a pencil?" he asked now.

She gave him a startled glance. Then smiled as if she was remembering the same moment in time. "Not so much," she said. "I usually make notes on my phone these days."

"Too bad."

"Sometimes I do it with the hair stick my dad got me when he was in Asia. It makes me feel closer to him."

Jace only nodded, because he couldn't think of a thing to say. A father who noticed such things as his child's small habits, enough to think of it when he was halfway around the world, was totally foreign to his experience. His own father couldn't have told anyone if he was right- or left-handed, let alone anything less obvious.

"What happened out there tonight, Jace?"

"You heard it."

"Yes, I did. Now I'd like to know what you didn't say."

"Nothing important."

"Oh, I'm sure if it was relevant you would have," she said. "Which means it was something else that had you so rattled."

"Maybe I was just afraid the guy would come after me."

"You're dodging."

Damn.

He'd forgotten that along with the smarts she was also very perceptive. She'd always known, when he'd arrived at their house, if he'd been having a particularly rough time with his father.

"Jace," she began again.

And stubborn.

When he finally gave in, he told himself it was only

because she already knew the history, thanks to him being unable to keep his mouth shut earlier.

"The guy got to his car and was jamming on the gas. Cutter was…right in front of him."

"My God," she breathed, her hand falling away from the key she'd put in the ignition. And he knew she understood. Max. He'd just told her the hideous truth about what had happened to his beloved pet, so she knew it was in the forefront of his mind.

"Jace," she said softly. "It's all right. He's all right. History didn't repeat itself."

His head came up sharply, his gaze snapping to her face. He wasn't sure if she'd helped or made him feel worse.

"I ran for him, but…if he hadn't come back when I yelled, he would have…"

"But he did." Her tone was gentle.

"Yeah. To keep me from falling apart like some wimpy head case." She looked back at the dog in the back seat. "Yeah," he said edgily, "he knew." He tried to describe what the dog had done, but what had seemed so obvious at the time sounded more than a little crazy now. "Never mind," he muttered.

"It makes perfect sense. Dogs are very perceptive about humans. And they're soothing. That's why there are therapy dogs, right? They just make you feel better."

Okay, that definitely made him feel worse. A therapy dog? She thought he needed that? "Yeah, right. And he knew I was going to be no help at all."

Cutter got to his feet in the back seat. His nose, a bit

cold, nudged Jace's cheek as Cassie said sharply, "Stop it, Jace. It had to be the most awful flashback for you."

"It was almost twenty years ago."

"And like yesterday. Things that horrible don't fade, we just don't think about them as often."

"Mm-hmm," he muttered, unable to think of anything else to say. She was being so understanding, so kind, it should be like a salve on the old wound, but instead it was just making him more aware of how he'd frozen out there. He could have put an end to this tonight, but instead he'd turned into that little kid, full of disbelief and horror. Useless. Worthless.

"What's your father's name?"

Startled, he snapped out of the painful thoughts and stared at her. "What?"

"Your father's first name was Charles, wasn't it?"

"Yeah. Chuck, he went by. Why?"

"Oh, that'll be good, because it rhymes with what I'd really want to say."

He felt a bit bewildered. Not the first time with her. "What?"

"Because whenever I catch you slipping back into believing all that crap he said to you, I'm going to say it."

He stared at her. He'd never seen her look more determined, even at nine when she'd been out to prove to Cory she could get up on the roof just like he could. And she had. She just hadn't been able to get down.

And trusted you enough to jump when you promised you'd catch her.

"You're not what he said you were," she said. "Not any of it."

"How do you know?"

"Because I know you."

He let out a compressed breath. "You don't know anything about who I am now."

Both her expression and her voice went gentle. "Don't I? That you're here tells me everything I need to know. You're a guy who came over a thousand miles to keep a promise."

As if that settled it, she reached down and started the car. And Jace realized that for Cassie, that did settle it.

"Thirsty, boy?" Cassidy asked.

Jace looked up from his paper as he sat at the kitchen counter; he'd been writing or doodling since they'd gotten home from the shop. He hadn't lost that habit, and she was glad. And if it made him feel better than he had been on the drive home, she was even gladder.

She smiled at him. "I meant the dog."

He glanced down to where Cutter was politely waiting as she set a fresh bowl of water on the floor. "Oh."

She watched the dog lap for a moment, then looked up at Jace. "If you are, too, I'll get you something. But there's no way anyone would call you a boy," she said. She saw something flicker in his eyes. Instinctively she knew he was remembering that flashback moment, when he must have felt like the helpless child he'd been. As if he'd sensed something, too, Cutter stopped drinking and his head came up.

"Chuck!"

He drew back sharply. "I didn't say anything."

"You were thinking it."

He looked disconcerted enough that she knew she'd been right. To emphasize her certainty, Cutter walked over to sit at Jace's feet and lean against his leg as he sat on the counter stool.

"Reading my mind now?" He ignored the dog and sounded on edge again.

"Mainly I was just testing to be sure it would register. From now on it's for real."

"Thanks. Just what I need, that name thrown in my face all the time."

"Then don't think like that all the time." Cutter, she saw, was leaning in harder, as if he knew Jace needed the touch. She kept going. "He was a cruel, vindictive man, Jace. And he was wrong, about everything. He doesn't deserve an ounce of your thought or memory."

She'd started out levelly enough, but by the time she finished, her voice had risen a notch. She couldn't help it. And her impassioned words seemed to echo in the room. He finally reached down to brush his fingers over Cutter's dark fur, but he kept his gaze on her. His expression changed as he looked at her, as if he were hearing that echo.

"Gonna save me, little girl?" he said softly.

Her breath caught. And that day so many years ago came back to her in a rush, when he'd said those same words to her. Her mother had picked her up from a playdate with a friend, and then Cory and Jace at the martial arts studio. They were late both because of traffic and because she and Tara had created a mess they had to clean up, with both her mother and Tara's father watching sternly.

As they'd finally pulled up to drop Jace off down the street, her mother had looked at him with concern.

"Will he be angry you're late?"

Jace, barely thirteen then, although he seemed much older to her, had shrugged. "He's always mad."

"I'll tell him about the traffic," her mother said soothingly.

"Won't matter. It'll still be my fault."

This had struck her, even at eleven, as grossly unfair. In the front seat, she had turned to look at him. "But it's not. It's my fault—Tara and I made a mess and we had to clean it up. And I'll tell him so."

Jace had looked so surprised she couldn't even guess what it meant. But then she knew, because he'd said those words in quiet amazement.

Gonna save me, little girl?

And he remembered, even now. How rare must it have been for someone to stand up for him that he so clearly remembered, over sixteen years later, an eleven-year-old doing it? And that he'd thought her that little girl when she was only two years younger than he was told her worlds about how old he felt inside. She thought her heart must be breaking.

"I would have done it back then," she said now, her voice as soft as his had been. "I would have told him."

"It wouldn't have made any difference. Even if he smiled and thanked you, he still would have blamed me once you were gone." He let out a breath. "And he would have found out what I was really doing those afternoons, and that would have been the end of it."

She let out a sigh, not of disbelief because she knew

it was true, but of incredulity because she couldn't understand how a parent could be like that. She'd been even luckier than she knew.

"I'm sorry, Jace. So sorry you had to grow up that way."

"Ancient history." He snapped out the words.

"It won't really be until you can let go of him. And all the damage he tried to do to you." She saw his jaw clench. The muscle jumped, as if he were fighting the tightness. Or as if he was fighting something else, something internal. "Maybe you should just let go and scream at him. Tell him everything that's piled up in your gut with his name on it."

He grimaced, staring down at the pen in his hand. "And what good would that do?"

"Catharsis?" she suggested.

"Yelling at somebody who's not there? I think that's a symptom of something. Not to mention pointless. Not that he'd listen if he was there."

Well, the bitter sarcasm was new. When she spoke again, her voice was very soft. "I don't give one single damn about him. I meant it might be good for you. You're the one I care about."

His head came up sharply. He started to turn his head to look at her, then stopped and looked away. She had the oddest feeling he didn't trust himself to look at her.

"I don't want your pity." He said it through clenched teeth.

"Good, because I don't have any to give you." What she did have to give him, he likely wouldn't want, either. "Are you angry at me?"

He let out a long, slow breath. "No." His mouth quirked wryly. "I don't have the energy."

Concern spiked through her. "Are you sick?"

"No. Just...tired."

Cassidy tilted her head, studying him. He looked perfectly healthy, better even, with those shoulders and chest. Lean, yes, but muscled, and he still moved with that subtle grace she'd always loved. No, there was nothing wrong with Jace Cahill, nothing at all.

"Why?"

"Never mind."

He said it flatly enough she knew he wasn't going any further. At least not now. He started to wad up the paper from the counter, but she got a glimpse, realized he'd been drawing on it, and grabbed it out of his hand. It was the caricature kind of thing he used to do, capturing the essence of the subject in a few clever, exaggerated lines. In this case Cutter, and she laughed aloud when she saw it.

"Oh, you've captured him perfectly! The ears, the tilt of his head, those wise eyes and the way he looks at you that starts you attributing all kinds of human traits to him."

He drew back slightly, staring at her. But he was almost smiling, one corner of his mouth twisting upward. "You, too, huh? He looks at you like he knows exactly how things should be, and you're the stupid one for not seeing it."

He looked down at the dog when he said it, and the dog lifted his head to meet Jace's gaze. For a moment neither moved, then Jace gave a slight shake of his head and a short chuckle.

"Amazing, isn't it?" she said, watching them. "I read somewhere that some people think herding dogs mesmerize the sheep with their eyes. He makes me believe it."

Jace started to smile, but it didn't quite make it all the way. His brow furrowed, and those blue eyes took on a distant look again, as if he were remembering something. She didn't think it was an unpleasant memory, for he looked more…puzzled. Doubtful. Something like that. So she didn't speak the name she'd chosen as a wake-up word.

She looked at the drawing again. Felt a pang that he apparently wasn't utilizing that talent. At least not in the way she'd always thought he would; when Mr. Gresham had suggested architecture, Jace had seemed excited by the idea.

She put the paper down on the counter and smoothed out the edges where he'd begun to crumple it. "Why on earth would you throw this away?"

"It's just a silly sketch."

"It's brilliant. If you don't want it, I do."

"All yours," he said, as if it were nothing. "What are you going to do, hang it on the fridge?"

"No, I'll add it to the collection." She said it before she thought, then turned her face away so he wouldn't see the color she could feel rising to her cheeks.

"Collection? You collect weird little drawings?"

Her head snapped back around. "No. And it's not weird!"

He half shrugged in an "If you say so" kind of way. And seized by a need to show him someone at least valued this talent of his, she slapped the page down on the counter, saying, "Don't you dare wad this up."

She went quickly to her room and grabbed a picture frame off the dresser, then went to the walk-in closet. She stood there for a moment, trying to remember where she'd put the box. She'd come across it when she'd moved into this room, had thought of tossing it, but ended up going through it and genuinely laughing for the first time since her parents had died, and she couldn't bring herself to do it.

She spotted the corner of the blue box that had once held file folders. She grabbed it, tugged it out from under the similar box that held old family photographs she kept meaning to scan into digital; she'd done a few of her parents but had run out of the emotional fuel to keep going.

She carried the box back into the kitchen. Jace was scratching Cutter's ears and looking quite a bit calmer. She set the box on the counter in front of him and pulled off the lid. He stared down at the not inconsiderable stack of papers, different shapes and colors, small and large, with only one thing in common. Each one held one of his quick, clever drawings, the things he had called silly and she had adored.

"Wha—" he began but stopped. Then tried again. "Where did you get all these?"

"You gave me some when I asked, remember?"

"Not this many," he said, still staring down at the box.

"I found some. I started looking around the house

after you'd been here. I even snuck into Cory's room to see if you'd left any there. And when I realized you put so little value on them you'd toss them, I started going through the paper trash."

His head came up slowly. He was staring at her with as much astonishment as he'd looked at the box. Slowly, his brow furrowed, and he gave a slight shake of his head.

"Why?" He sounded as astonished as he'd looked.

Before he could make any assumptions, she said quickly, "I saved these because they were good, not because I had a crush on you. Although I did."

"They're just...doodles."

"After my parents were killed, it was too hard to have our family photo where I would see it all the time."

He frowned, clearly puzzled by the apparent non sequitur. "I saw it, out there," he said, gesturing toward the living room. "But—"

"What I do have, in my room, where I can see it every day, is this."

She held out the frame to him. She saw his eyes widen as he realized what it was. The caricature-style sketch he'd done that brilliant summer day, when they'd had a backyard barbecue and he'd been allowed to stay because his father was out of town, was one of her most precious possessions. She'd often thought it would be one of the things she would grab first in a fire.

It was more detailed than his usual quick work, as if he'd put more time into it. And in the process he'd captured the very essence of the two people she'd loved most in the world—her mother's warmth and kindness and beauty, her father's strength and steadiness and honesty. But more than that, and more important to her, he'd captured the magic between them, in her father's rather rakish grin and the twinkle in her mother's eyes as they looked at each other.

"I remember this," he said, staring at it. "Your parents… I'd never seen anything like how they looked at each other. I don't think I even knew what it meant, only that it was there."

And that, Cassidy thought, was one of the saddest things about this clever portrait of two people who so obviously adored each other. The artist hadn't recognized what he was seeing, because he'd never seen it before.

He'd never seen parents who actually loved each other.

Chapter 11

Jace sat staring at the image from that long-ago day. He remembered wondering why he kept coming to the Grants'. It was respite from the misery at home, yes, but it also made that misery seem even worse when he saw what they had.

"I almost punched Cory out that day," he said, lost in memory and barely aware of speaking aloud.

"He probably had it coming, but why?" Cassie asked, her voice so quiet it didn't jerk him out of his thoughts.

"Because he didn't appreciate what he had."

"I think it was more he took it for granted."

He looked at her then. There was understanding in her eyes, but nothing of sympathy or pity, and so he could go on. "But you didn't."

She shook her head. "It was your life that taught me. I saw what you were going through, and it showed me how lucky we were. But Cory is...oblivious, sometimes."

He managed a wry smile. "I've noticed."

She sighed. "I'd hoped he'd step up, to help with the

shop, but he said he couldn't live tied to a daily grind."
She grimaced. "As if I love it."

Jace couldn't stop the harsh, sharp breath that escaped him. Daily grind? He could tell Cory a thing or
two about that.

"I know," she said. "Cory always looks for the easy
way. You never had an easy way. And that's not pity,"
she added before he could speak. "It's the truth and
you know it."

He made a noncommittal sound, trying to think of a
way to divert her. Seeing that image made him remember drawing it, with that hollow ache inside. He'd been
glad the Grants let him into their lives as much as they
had, but it had made him hate going home even more.

"Others have had it worse," he finally said.

"Because he didn't actually hit you? You think that's
the only way damage is done?"

He couldn't talk about this. Not now, not with her.
"Cassie, please. This is all old news. Can we concen-
trate on your problem now?"

He felt Cutter move, glanced down in time to see
the dog step behind Cassie, then apparently change his
mind and turn around. In the process he bumped her.
She took a step to catch her balance. A step toward him.

Damn, she was so close. And when she looked up
at him, those amazing eyes full of all the things she
wasn't saying, when she reached up to touch his face,
he thought he—

She kissed him.

Oh, not a hot, wet, "I'm hungry for you" kiss, no, that
was all on his side. This was something softer, gentler,

even tender. And it made him ache inside in the same way he had the day he'd done that drawing. Then heat began to build deep and low inside him as his body let him know in no uncertain terms that it liked this. Liked it a lot.

And when she pulled back, it was all he could do not to protest. And he couldn't stop himself from wishing she still had that crush on him. Because this was not the girl he remembered—this Cassie was all woman. More woman than he'd ever known.

"That," she said, "was for this drawing, for giving me that wonderful memory to help fight off the pain."

He stared at her, his thoughts so jumbled now he suspected if he tried to talk he'd say something stupid or utterly nonsensical. She picked up the framed drawing and headed back to her room. He felt the strongest urge to follow her but made himself stay put; him alone with Cassie in her bedroom was not the wisest course just now.

He realized he was staring after her and forcibly shifted his gaze. It ended up on Cutter, who was sitting there looking up at him, and the only word that came to Jace's mind for his expression was *smug*. How could a dog look so pleased with himself? An image flashed through his mind, of that aborted movement the animal had made that had inadvertently pushed Cassie to him. It was inadvertent, wasn't it?

He was saved from further silly imaginings by the buzz of the Foxworth phone. He answered gratefully.

"Everything peaceful there?"

Depends on what you mean by peaceful. "Yeah. Fine."

"Take Cutter for a walk. Just you. North two blocks. Third-base side of the ball field in the park."

"I… Okay." He opened his mouth to ask why but realized there was no one there.

The moment he got the leash, Cutter was at his side, sitting politely but clearly expectantly. He clipped the lead on his collar. He hesitated. If he called out to Cassie, she might want to come along. And while he'd like that—maybe—Rafe had said alone. So he grabbed the pad of paper she'd made her list on before and scribbled her a note that he was taking the dog to the park. After a moment's thought, instead of signing it he added a little sketch at the bottom, of himself as he imagined he'd looked when he'd opened that box of drawings, wide-eyed and eyebrows shooting upward.

Cutter did indeed have good leash manners, walking at his side nicely, not pulling or tugging. They were there in less than five minutes from when Rafe had called. But there was no sign of the man from Foxworth.

For a moment he just stood there, looking at the baseball diamond in the park where he'd once played. And only once—his father had put a halt to the activity the moment Jace made the mistake of saying how much fun it was in the man's hearing.

He managed not to jump, barely, when Rafe appeared to his left as if he'd just materialized there. There were no niceties, except between Rafe and Cutter; the dog greeted him happily and he leaned to stroke his ears.

When he straightened, his voice came rapid-fire, startling Jace.

"Ten seconds. Tell me who pops into your mind as the most likely person to bring trouble into her life."

Startled, Jace was sure he was gaping. "I…"

"Five seconds."

Jace held up his hands in a helpless gesture. "I… All I can think of is Cory."

"Her brother."

"Yes. He sometimes skates on the edge." Even as he said it, he was shaking his head. "But he loves her. And he has always been protective of her."

"And if he was desperate?"

"He would never intentionally do anything that would hurt her." Jace said it with a certainty he felt about few things in life anymore.

"But unintentionally?"

"I…don't know."

"His record doesn't show much. Drunk in public, fights and a couple of petty thefts."

Jace grimaced. "That's just what he got caught at."

"Figured there was more."

"He stole a car once. He was damned proud of himself, too. Even brought it over, wanted me to go for a joyride. But he chickened out and took it back, and the owner never knew who did it."

"And what did you tell him when he wanted you to join him?"

"I told him to get the hell out. I had enough problems, no way I was getting sucked into that."

"Interesting. A lot of kids in your position would have gone that way."

Jace met his gaze then. "I couldn't do that to my mom. She was barely hanging on as it was." When Rafe didn't speak but only looked at him, he felt compelled to add, "She did her best. She's…small. Delicate. But she still tried to divert him when he started in on me. She'd take it herself, but she hated that he kept telling me how stupid and worthless I was."

He heard a tiny sound and spun around. Cassie was behind him, staring at him, pain in her eyes. And sympathy. God, he hated that. But no shock or surprise, so she couldn't have heard the part about Cory's aborted grand theft auto escapade. He'd never told anyone, because he'd promised Cory he wouldn't, as long as it never happened again. But now he had to weigh Cassie's welfare against that promise, and it was no contest.

Promises. He needed to be a lot more careful about throwing those around, obviously.

"I saw your note, so I thought I'd…" Her voice trailed away, and she shifted her gaze to Rafe. "Should I not have come?"

"I'm as sure as I can be that he's not around at the moment," Rafe said. "But next time, stay put."

And safe, Jace thought.

"I hate this…helpless feeling!"

"Sucks," Rafe said succinctly. Then he glanced at the very utilitarian-looking watch he wore. "Spend some time here with him," he said, indicating Cutter. He reached into a pocket and pulled out, of all things, a rather worse-for-wear tennis ball and held it out to

Jace. "Throw this for him, make it look like that's the reason you're here. We'll be in touch."

Jace took the ball, and without another word Rafe nodded at Cassie and was gone. Moments later he disappeared into the trees at the edge of the ball field.

"*We'll* be in touch?" Cassie said, staring after him.

"Maybe the guy he's got working on the video."

"Oh." Then, with a tentative smile, "I liked the drawing. It's the only one I have that's actually of you."

He grimaced. "I don't usually try to draw myself."

She looked at him for a moment before saying quietly, "No. You wouldn't."

He wasn't sure what that was supposed to mean, but he was glad enough that she wasn't talking about what she'd walked up on that he didn't dwell on it.

Half an hour later, he was staring at Cutter as he brought the more gray than yellow tennis ball back for...he'd lost count of how many times.

"Dang, dog, don't you ever get tired?"

"Or ever miss?" Cassie added. They'd discovered that while Jace had the advantage on distance, she had been able to add some amazing spins to her throws, keeping the dog guessing as to which way the ball was really going to go. Yet he never missed, sometimes twisting himself practically double to make a spectacular catch.

"He should sleep well tonight, at least," Jace said. *Which would make him one up on me.*

He heard a buzz. Her Foxworth phone. She handed him the ball and pulled it out of her jacket pocket.

Looked at the screen and laughed. Then she held it up for him to see. A text from the laconic Rafe.

He likes carrots, if you've got them.

They started back. Jace had intended to keep Cutter between them, but the dog insisted not only on walking on the outside, but on continuously bumping him, as if he was trying to nudge him ever closer to Cassie. And he didn't quit until they got back to the house. Once inside, Cassie went to the refrigerator, dug out a carrot and snapped it into small pieces for him. He watched the dog take them politely and chomp them with obvious gusto.

He was, Jace thought, a very different dog. Sometimes just a playful animal, but other times... That made him think about Rafe's comment about him herding the stalker—or whatever he was—into the light so Jace could get that video. He laughed inwardly; the dog was obviously very clever, but that was a bit much. Wasn't it?

He was saved from that insanity-inducing thought by a buzz from the Foxworth phone in his back pocket at the same time Cassie's buzzed from the jacket she'd tossed over one of the stools at the counter. He pulled his phone out. Someone—the message was identified with the name Ty Hewitt—had sent them and Rafe a photo. Jace studied it for a moment, trying to see the man he'd encountered earlier—and let get away—in the image.

Possible, he thought. And it did look like the guy in the video, although the angle was different. Then he heard Cassie walk over and glanced up to see she held her phone and was looking at the image as well.

"Is that a mug shot?" she asked.

"Looks like."

"It kind of looks like him, around the mouth and nose. But I can't be sure, I haven't seen his face clearly enough. And he was always bundled up, so I wouldn't have seen that tattoo on his neck anyway."

"Yeah." *Maybe that's why he was always wrapped up like he was in Alaska.*

The phones buzzed in unison as a text came through.

Pic only a 72% match thru facial rec. Still on it for a closer hit.

A moment later Rafe had texted back, Copy. Advise.

And then Cassie's phone rang. She answered quickly, and at Rafe's instruction, turned on the speaker and set it down in front of them both.

"You got the photo?"

"Yes, we did," Cassie said.

"Opinions?"

They told him.

"Who is he?" Cassie asked.

"Name's Al Schiff. He's from Seattle. Part of a local criminal enterprise there, with quite a record. Petty theft to drugs to armed robbery."

Jace looked up from the phone just as Cassie did the same. She looked as if she'd felt the same chill he had; he hadn't expected that.

"But…there's no reason someone like that would come after me," she protested.

"He didn't. He's just the closest match Ty's come up with so far, so I wanted you to look at him."

"Oh." Cassie hesitated and then said, "I could be wrong, I don't think I ever saw his eyes, but…"

"You may have seen more than you realize," Rafe said. "What?"

"I just had the impression he has lighter eyes than this man. But I can't be sure."

Jace looked back at the photo on his phone. This man indeed had dark eyes. But Cassie's uncertainty brought back the first question that had occurred to him at Rafe's prior words.

"How can you be so sure it isn't him?"

"Because he's sitting in prison at the moment."

Cassidy's thoughts were jumbled. At first she'd felt the oddest combination of disquiet and relief. The former was easy to understand; connecting what was going on to some guy in prison was unsettling, whether true or not.

The second, the relief, was about something she'd buried from the moment this had started. That possibility she'd worked so hard to deny. But if somebody in prison was behind this, then she could face it. Her brother might not be the most successful, upstanding guy, but he would never get involved with someone like this.

But if this guy was in prison, then he wasn't the man stalking her. So maybe he wasn't connected at

all. Maybe the two men just happened to look similar.
It happened.

She gave her head a sharp shake.

"Just confused the issue, didn't it?" Jace said after
Rafe had hung up with his usual lack of niceties.

She looked up from the phone on the counter. "Yes."

"Maybe this Ty will find a closer match. Maybe this
guy has nothing to do with any of this."

She drew in a deep breath. "I confess, I didn't expect
anything this soon anyway. You've only been here…
two days."

Two days. Two days and Jace had turned her life up-
side down. Had her thinking of so many things, had her
usually orderly thoughts and feelings in a tangled mess.
And then, of course, to top it off, she'd kissed him.

And scared the heck out of herself.

She'd meant it only as a thank-you, for the drawing
that had truly helped her cope, but it had very nearly
become much, much more. As a teenager she'd fantasized about kissing him. But those fantasies had been
childish, ignorant things. The heat that had sparked in
her at that brief touch had burned away all semblance
of fantasy; it had been Jace, the real Jace, and she'd had
to pull away before she embarrassed them both by turning a thank-you into something else entirely.

And yet she ached, truly ached to do it again. For
real this time. Not as a thank-you but as a woman to a
man she wanted to—

The ring of the house phone cut off her thoughts,
which was probably just as well. She used the landline so rarely sometimes she even forgot it was there,

but she kept it because many of her parents' friends had the number and she didn't want to cut them out by dropping it.

She went to the living room and grabbed the receiver from the charger on a back corner of an end table.

"Cassidy?" It was a female voice that was vaguely familiar.

"Yes?"

"This is Elizabeth Cahill. Jace's mom."

"Hello!" she exclaimed. "How are you?"

"Very well, thanks. How are you? I hope your problem is getting resolved."

"I think it's getting there." She started walking back toward the kitchen. "Thank you for…the loan."

The woman laughed, and Cassidy thought she'd never heard her sound so…light. But her voice went serious, sincere when she said, "I was so sorry about your parents, Cassidy. They were good, sweet, generous people."

"Yes. Yes, they were."

"They helped my boy so much. More than I ever did."

It sounded so much like Jace when he was down on himself that she was tempted to say something to this quiet, small woman she remembered as always being sad. But she didn't sound sad now. In fact, she sounded quite upbeat.

"Is he there?" Elizabeth asked. "I wanted to give him some good news."

"I'm all for that," she said, meaning it.

She'd reached Jace now. She held out the phone, and he gave her a startled look. "It's your mom. She says she has good news," she added quickly.

He took the phone quickly then. "Mom?" A pause. "I'm fine. What's your news?"

Cassidy walked back to her bedroom to give him some privacy. She had some things to put away in the bathroom anyway. But instead of tidying the counter where she'd left makeup and her hairbrush tossed— and she had not spent more time than usual on that this morning just because Jace was here, it was only because she hadn't slept well and she'd been trying to mask the damage—she found herself in the bedroom staring at the drawing again.

She wondered why he hadn't pursued that dream of being an architect. She remembered hearing her parents discussing it late one night when she'd been up studying for finals her junior year, wondering if it was because they couldn't afford the schooling or his father simply wouldn't let him.

His father's parents must have been awful, to turn out a man like that.

She remembered her mother's words so clearly. And her father's answer. *Most parents want their kids to have it better than they did. Charles Robinson seems to want Jace to have it harder than he did...*

Cassidy remembered thinking about their words long after she should have been back to studying. For the first time in her young life, she'd really thought about what it must be like to have parents like that. Tried to imagine her own father saying she couldn't have or do something just because he never could. She couldn't picture it. He might tell her she'd have to work for it, or pay for it herself, but saying no for that kind of reason? Never.

But she could picture Jace's father saying it. And later, when her mother had checked on her before they'd gone to bed, she'd tossed down her history notes and run to hug her.

And she had to stifle a sudden urge to go hug Jace now.

You already kissed the guy, isn't that enough?

She almost laughed aloud at the little voice in her head. No, it wasn't enough. That was the problem. Poor Jace, he'd come here to help her, to keep a promise to Cory, and Cory's little sister plants one on him, as if she were the same girl who had a crush on him all those years ago.

She wasn't the same girl. But apparently her taste was the same, because Jace was the prototype for every guy she'd ever been attracted to.

And now the original is here, under your roof, sleeping in your old room. And half the reason you're not sleeping is because you're thinking about sneaking down the hall to him and—

She cut off her own thought when she realized the murmuring that had been all she could hear from the other room had stopped. She reached out to touch the framed drawing, then left her bedroom.

He had already replaced the handset in the charger and was still in the living room, staring out the front window into the night. She hesitated but saw he was smiling. And that Cutter was not leaning against him, offering comfort, but had curled up on one end of the couch, the spot she had patted and urged him up on earlier, to let him know it was okay.

She walked over to Jace. "So it really was good news?"

"Yes. Very."

"For her, or you?"

"Both."

"I'm glad," she said simply.

Later, just as she was falling asleep, she remembered what he'd said last night. *She needed help. I couldn't just walk away from her.*

Just like he'd come to her when she needed help.

That night her mind manufactured a crazy, convoluted dream that involved the man in the hoodie morphed into Jace's father, her and Jace's mother hiding in some kind of deserted building, and Jace riding up like some white knight, except in the dream he was on a motorcycle, Cutter somehow keeping up with him next to the powerful machine. That at least made sense, she thought when she woke up; he'd always wanted a motorcycle. Well, and maybe Cutter; that dog was full of surprises. She had the feeling keeping pace with a motorcycle might be the least of them.

Almost as if her thoughts had conjured him, the dog slipped through the door that was open just enough to let him through. He seemed happiest if he could spend part of the night with each of them, so he went back and forth from here to the guest room.

And not for the first time she had to quash the obvious thought—it would be easier on the dog if they were together.

Just the thought of waking up with Jace made her shiver, even in the warmth of her bed. She chalked it up to Cutter's cold nose bumping her cheek. "Time to get up, huh?" she asked, pulling a hand free to scratch the dog's ear. "You wake him up yet?"

The dog let out a sigh that sounded very weary, and she laughed at herself when her brain went back to her thought of a moment ago.

"Aw, that hallway too long for you, lazybones?" she asked as she sat up, then yawned. "At least you're not growling, so I guess the creeper isn't around."

May was opening the shop today, so she didn't have to rush through her shower. She did anyway, to make sure there was enough hot water for Jace. At least she'd slept a little better, crazy dreams notwithstanding. Of course, any sleep at all would be better than the night before.

When she went out into the kitchen she found a tousled, sleepy-eyed Jace at the coffeemaker. She'd shown him where everything was, and they'd agreed first one up would start it. She'd forgotten that.

She went to get coffee mugs from the cupboard, noticing the drip of the dark liquid into the pot was slowing. "Sorry. I should have started that before I took my shower."

He froze in place, as if she'd said something stunning. It was a moment before he answered, without turning around. "I was first up."

"You were?"

"Unless you were up before five, yes."

What happened to the guy who liked to stay up late and sleep in?

Reality.

"Anything from Rafe?" she asked as she nudged a mug over to him.

"He called a little after five. He said he'd be talking to some people this morning." He picked up the pot and filled the mugs. Hers first, she noticed.

"Good idea," she said briskly. "Since May is opening today and I don't have to be there until noon, we can do the same."

He gave her a sideways look and a slight frown. "The same?"

"Talk."

He looked pained. "Oh."

She nearly laughed at him. "It's not so hard. We'll start with something easy. Like what have you been doing? Why are you used to getting up so early? What was your mom's good news?"

He picked up his coffee and turned to face her, leaning against the counter. "You missed your calling. You could be a pushy reporter."

"I think that's a redundancy," she said with a teasing smile. But the smile faded as she added, "I guess we both missed our calling. Or rather, neither of us got to pursue it."

"I always figured you'd end up a college professor or something."

She wrinkled her nose. "Are you trying to say I tried to instruct too much? Or just that I was a know-it-all?"

"No. But you did always seem to know…everything. You used to amaze me, coming up with stuff I'd never even heard of."

"Thank you, but that's just reading," she said with a laugh.

"You always did have a book or a reader in your hand, seems like."

"Yes. And that was slick."

"What was?"

"Your diversion."

He lowered his gaze, studied the coffee mug before he took a sip. Cassidy let out a sigh.

"I'm sorry if my questions were pushy. If you feel your life is none of my business, just say so. I was just curious. I—we lost track of you after you left your aunt's."

He went very still. Then, slowly, he looked up at her. "I know. I missed your letters."

"I didn't think you even read them. Your mom answered emails, but you never did."

He answered like he was walking through a minefield. "I read them. Or she told me about them."

"But you never—"

"I didn't have time, all right?" he snapped. "She worked close to the library, so she'd go use their computers to check mail at lunch."

Cassidy heard Cutter make a low sound, but she didn't look at the dog. Dominoes were falling in her mind. No computer at home to check? No phone? She stared at him, feeling like a fool. It had finally clicked in her head.

They're going to live with Elizabeth's sister.

It'll be rough for them, the way Chuck left them.

She'd been so stupid. She'd been wrapped up in her

life, finals, her senior year in high school coming up, when they'd moved. It had made perfect sense to her that they'd move in with Jace's aunt when his father had left. Her own aunt had stayed with them for a few months after her divorce until she got herself situated. What had puzzled her was why anyone would think they wouldn't be better off without Jace's domineering, cruel father.

Money. It was his father's income they had been talking about.

"I'm sorry, Jace. I'm a spoiled idiot, and I don't blame you for not wanting to share personal things with me." Cutter whined now. She seized on the chance for escape. "I think he needs out. I'll take him."

She grabbed the leash from the table by the door, clipped it on the dog's collar and stepped outside into the light but steady rain. The dog hung back, looking at Jace, who was staring down into that coffee mug as if it held the answer to all the mysteries of the universe.

She had never felt more humbled in her life.

Chapter 12

The sound of the door closing behind her snapped Jace out of his self-pity-fest. Cassie was heading outside with only Cutter. No wonder the dog had whined. At least he remembered what Jace's job here was. He ran across the room, grabbed up his jacket as he went after her.

She hadn't even made it out to the sidewalk yet. She didn't look back, and something about the way her voice had sounded when she'd left made him slow a little. He was close enough to get to her in a couple of seconds, and he trusted Cutter to handle those seconds. Which was a good thing, because right now he doubted she wanted him anywhere near her.

Right now all you have is how you present yourself, Jace.

His mother's advice, given when they were so far under he didn't think they'd ever see the surface again, echoed in his head. Along with the knowledge that he'd just presented himself as a complete jerk.

He didn't know if she knew he was there. She kept walking. Along the path he'd taken so often as a kid, from the house where most of the happier moments of his young life had happened toward the house where the unpleasant rest of it had been spent. How could Cory not treasure what he'd had? How could he take it so for granted that he abused the privilege of having a safe home and two solid, reliable, loving parents? And how could he careen so wildly with this as his center?

Tell me who pops into your mind as the most likely person to bring trouble into her life.

Rafe's abrupt question echoed in his head. And he hated that the answer was still the same.

It was the change in Cutter that alerted her, otherwise she never would have realized Rafe was there, he moved so silently. When the dog's head came up and his tail wagged, she knew it wasn't a threat. And it wasn't Jace, because he was probably still in the house wondering why he'd ever bothered to try to help such a spoiled, oblivious fool. So when she turned around and Rafe was right there, a cup of coffee in his hand, she at least wasn't shocked.

"Do you ever sleep?" she asked as he bent to greet the happy dog. Then, before he could say anything, she held up a hand. "Never mind. It's apparently my morning for thoughtless prying."

The man didn't answer, just gave her a questioning look and waited.

"Jace," she admitted. "I very stupidly missed something that should have been obvious, about why they moved away. And I poked at him about it, as if everybody in the world had the good luck to grow up the way I did."

"Good you're aware. What should have been obvious?"

"I think they moved because they were…in financial trouble after his father walked out." His gaze shifted, looking over her shoulder, but his expression never even flickered. "You knew," she said flatly.

He looked back at her. "We do background checks on potential clients. People lie."

She suppressed a sigh, one of exasperation at herself. "Jace doesn't. Unless it's lies of omission."

"Everybody's entitled to some secrets."

Something in the way he said it made her wonder what secrets this man held close. Probably to keep fools like her from making assumptions.

"When he first got here, I was…surprised," Cassidy said. "He always had such plans—he was going to be an architect, design great buildings. But he didn't go after his dream."

"That's because a nightmare came after him."

She blinked. "What?"

He held her gaze for a long moment, as if he were pondering whether or not to tell her something. Then he did that glance over her shoulder again. It must be habit, she thought. Finally, he said, "His father had run up a ton of bills, including gambling debts and a second mortgage on the house that he hadn't paid in months. Well into six figures' worth of credit card debt. All of it jointly."

Cassidy stared at him. "They lost the house, didn't they."

It wasn't really a question, so he didn't answer, only nodded. "From what Ty—he's our tech guy and background researcher—found out, Jace's mother worked two jobs, and Jace worked three until they paid it off."

Her eyes widened. "They paid it all off?"

"Except the house, obviously. They let it go to foreclosure because they had no choice."

Cassidy vaguely remembered her parents talking about a foreclosure sale in the neighborhood, but she'd been getting ready to go away to college and hadn't really paid attention. *Too full of yourself to worry about anyone else back then.*

"They negotiated payoffs with all the credit cards, and it took them nearly eight years, but they did it."

She shook her head slowly. "But if it wasn't their debt, why didn't they just file for bankruptcy?"

"Pride, maybe. Or not wanting anyone to know what he'd done. In either case, apparently that's not in their lexicon." He said it admiringly.

Cassidy thought of tiny, quiet Elizabeth Rob— Cahill. She never would have guessed there was such a steel spine in that delicate-seeming woman. But she must have found it once she was out from under Chuck Robinson's thumb.

"And it's not every adult son who would put his life on hold to help his mother get out of a hole like that," Rafe added.

Slowly, thoughtfully, she nodded. "Jace would."

"Just like he would keep a promise made years ago."

"Yes," she said softly.

Call Jace. He'll come. He promised.

Even Cory, who broke promises so easily himself, had known that bedrock truth, that if Jace gave his word, it was golden. How had that happened? How had the boy who'd had such a sterling example in their father turned out to be so unreliable, while the boy whose father had apparently been a cruel, heedless reprobate had turned out so…sterling?

"No wonder he seems tired," she said.

"Wears on you." Rafe's expression changed this time as he looked past her shoulder once more. She felt a surge of alarm, but a glance at Cutter soothed it. The dog's tail was wagging again. "But not so tired that he forgot why he was here," Rafe added quietly. He made a gesture, as if waving someone over. "He's been here all along, you know. He was right behind you the whole time."

She barely stopped herself from whirling around. She'd truly been oblivious, of more things than one. She closed her eyes for a moment. "I'm such a fool."

"No." Rafe's quiet denial made her look at him. "A fool never thinks himself a fool." Somehow, coming from this man, that was tantamount to the highest praise. "Besides," he added, "you've learned quickly to trust Cutter."

She remembered her glance at the dog and how it had assured her there wasn't a threat. She couldn't help but smile.

And then Jace was there. So quickly she knew he'd been close. She should have known better than to think he would let her wander around alone. Even with Cutter.

Rafe nodded. The now familiar Foxworth notification buzzed, but only on Rafe's phone. "You should head back now," he said.

That quickly he turned away, the phone up to his ear. Cassidy just looked at Jace. Now that she knew, she felt even more foolish for not putting together the signs. The slightly frayed clothes, the weariness in and around his eyes. He was lean but solid now, but still she wondered if he'd been too thin, with no time to eat, or if even food had been limited in those years.

She waited until there was no one nearby, with what Rafe had told her rolling around in her mind, before she said anything. And then, when they were halfway home, she did it quickly, wanting it out before it ate up her stomach.

"I apologize, Jace. I didn't know, and I was too blind to realize. All I knew was that you'd gone. I was too self-focused then to worry much about why, other than your father had left."

He stopped dead on the sidewalk at the corner of her block. He was staring at her, and he didn't look happy. But she went on, feeling she had to get it said.

"I didn't know what you and your mom were dealing with. I wouldn't have understood then anyway, really, because I was so...protected, but—"

"What," he said rather sharply, "is it you think you know?"

"About your father leaving you in such debt."

He drew back. His jaw tightened. "Rafe."

"Yes."

"For a guy who doesn't talk much, he sure talked to you."

"Don't blame him, please. I had already guessed, finally, he just told me how...bad it was."

"Great."

"I don't blame you for being angry."

"I'm not angry."

"You should be. I was prying into things you didn't want to tell me."

The tightness in his voice exploded. "I didn't tell you," he said, enunciating far too carefully, "because you'd feel sorry for me—"

"I wouldn't—"

"—and sympathy is not what I want from you."

For a moment she just stared at him. His jaw was set, as if he were fighting some internal battle.

She had to moisten her lips to speak. To ask. She thought—no, hoped—she knew the answer. But she had to ask it anyway.

"What do you want from me?"

For an instant he didn't answer her. He just stared at her, those amazing blue eyes lit with something she'd never seen in them before. On the periphery of her vision, she saw movement, knew it was Cutter. The dog had, oddly, come up behind Jace and seemed to be nudging him in that way he had. But she didn't, couldn't look away from those eyes, realized she was barely breathing as she waited for him to answer her question.

And then he did, in the most basic, elemental way possible.

His mouth came down on hers fiercely, hungrily, as if he'd been holding this in his mind since the day he'd left town. This was not the brotherly kissing away of her tears, or the restrained, sweet, thankful kiss she'd given him. This was something wild, uncontrolled, demanding.

This was the kiss she had always wanted from him, even when she'd been too young to understand the foolish longings in her heart. This was a calling, a claiming, and every nerve in her body answered joyously. And she knew that this, this was what had been missing in every relationship she'd tried to have. They hadn't worked because this fire hadn't been there. They hadn't worked because her heart hadn't been wholly in it.

They hadn't worked because it hadn't been Jace.

There was no one around, but they were out in public. He didn't care. He couldn't get enough of the taste of her. Caution told him to go slowly, to savor, but he wanted more, wanted the deepest, sweetest taste of her more than he'd ever wanted anything in his life. For an instant he had the crazy thought that the fates were here with them, saying, "Oops, we made a mistake—*this* is the life you should have had."

He stroked his tongue over the even ridge of her teeth. Felt a shudder when she let the tip of her tongue meet his. His pulse was starting to hammer, and it was getting harder to breathe. He deepened the kiss, hungrily, heedless now of any need for a gentler touch. He wanted this, wanted her, more than he'd ever wanted anything. She was the gold ring, the treasure just out of reach, all the things he'd never had, ever wanted and done without, all wrapped up into one.

It was, probably inevitably, she who broke the kiss. He hungrily reached for more, but she had pulled away.

"Let…let me catch my breath," she whispered, and

only the stunned, shaken sound of her voice let him hold back.

He was panting himself as he answered, "You should have plenty. You've got all of mine."

It was a stupid thing to say, silly, but it made her look up at him and smile. "You always did have a way of putting things," she said softly.

"Cassie," he said, not knowing what else to say, not having the breath anyway, and hating that it came out sounding like a pleading moan.

"You're the only one I ever let call me that, you know."

He blinked. "What?"

"Cassidy or Cass, that's for the rest of the world. Cassie was only for you."

"But... I've always called you that."

"Yes. And I stopped anyone else from using it from the first time you did."

Even then, as kid, she'd kept that separate? For him? That easily she nearly put him on his knees.

"I didn't know. I don't... I can't... I don't know what to say to you." He still sounded like he'd run a marathon.

"I can think of several appropriate things," she said. "Starting with *wow*."

And suddenly he could breathe again. "I was thinking of something maybe a bit more reverential. Like sayings that start with *holy*."

When she laughed and held his gaze while doing so, he wanted to hang on to this moment, to keep it, hold it just like it was this instant, to carry with him forever.

Pay attention. Every little detail. Freeze it, etch it into your mind, because this may be all you get.

"I've missed you, Jace Cahill," she said. "So much."

"I—"

Cutter's trumpeting bark cut him off. The dog burst into a run at the same instant, jerking the leash free. Head down and ears flattened, he was headed for the house.

For an instant he thought of telling Cassie to stay here, but he knew she wouldn't. It was her home the dog was headed for, something at her home that sparked that unmistakable warning. Intruder. And when he started to follow the dog at a run, she was right there, almost keeping pace.

They reached the front walk. Cutter had dashed around toward the backyard. And again Jace thought of telling her to stay here but knew she wouldn't. Better she was with him, anyway, than out here alone in case the guy came this way.

"Stay behind me," he ordered as they reached the side gate, where Cutter was clawing his way over the fence. He gave a ferocious snarl as he cleared the fence. Jace was right behind him, yanking the gate open. He heard a man's shout. He hit the corner of the house just in time to see a figure scrambling madly over the back fence toward the alley.

He ran, catching up with Cutter, who was trying to hurl himself over that much-higher fence. Jace heard the sound of a motor as he grabbed the top of the fence and hoisted himself up in time to see the same car as before pulling away.

He dropped back down and tried to calm the angry animal. "It's okay, boy. You warned us." He stroked the soft ears, but while the dog calmed, he clearly was not happy and set himself to sniffing every inch of the small backyard. And Jace saw the broken window in the back door, which stood ajar.

He pulled out his phone and hit the red button. "I need your keys," he said to her, jerking her attention away from the obvious entry point on the house. Her home. She started to dig them out of her pocket.

Rafe, as usual, skipped the formalities. "Go."

"He was inside. Same guy, same car. Dark gray. Headed south out of her alley." Then, with some satisfaction, he rattled off the complete license number; he'd seen the whole thing this time, in the daylight. Cassie handed him her keys. "I'll take Cassie's car and—"

"Stay with her. I'll look."

"But—"

"Call the sheriff. There's evidence now."

He hadn't thought of that yet. Still, it took an effort to tamp down the adrenaline and not give chase. "All right," he agreed. "Can I tell them about you?"

"Foxworth, yes. Be in touch."

Jace quickly explained to Cassie. She only nodded. She was staring at the broken window and the back door that stood ajar. He made the call to the sheriff's office, and to make it simpler kept it merely to the break-in they'd just interrupted. Time enough for the rest when they got here. They took the license plate number and said they'd put it out right away and have a deputy en route.

"I'm afraid to go in," Cassie admitted softly when he'd hung up.

"Don't blame you."

She took a step that way then stopped when he put

a hand on her arm. "I think we should we wait. You know, crime scene?"

"Oh. Yes. Of course." She stood there, still staring, her brow furrowed deeply. "I… The window. I'll need…"

"I'll handle it. Board it up for now, then we'll get it replaced."

She was silent for a long moment before she said, "Do you think he was…watching us? That he waited until we left?" He thought that was very likely true, but he didn't want her thinking about this creep watching her at home.

"Don't know." He'd have to ask the neighbors if they'd seen the guy. Or maybe the deputy would do that.

Cassie rubbed her hands up and down her arms. It wasn't that cold despite the rain, and he suspected she was more rattled than she let on. And then, without having made a conscious decision to do it, he closed the foot between them and put his arms around her. He knew by the way she turned to face him, the way she let out a tiny sigh as she leaned into him, that it had been the right move. But he wasn't sure what else to do to reassure her.

He felt a sudden weight on his right foot. He glanced down and saw Cutter had, of all things, sat on his boot. The dog was looking up at him pointedly.

"Yeah, you did good, dog." The animal's tail wagged slightly, but he shifted his gaze to Cassie. And suddenly Jace had a thought. "Boy," he said, as lightly as he could manage, "it's a good thing we had Cutter with us. If he hadn't warned us, we could have walked right in on the guy."

He heard Cassie take in a sharp breath. Then her

head came up, and as much as he missed the feel of it pressed against his chest, he was glad to see that her expression had changed. Her eyes were wide now.

"We could have. We really could have." She bent to the dog and stroked his head. "Thank you," she said, sounding completely different now, calmer, less shaken. And Jace couldn't help wondering if that had been the dog's plan. He seemed to know that petting him could calm people, so why wouldn't he be able to figure out how to get that done?

Sure, and maybe he planted the right words in your head, too?

When the sheriff's deputy arrived, she was brisk, efficient and thorough. Jace could tell Cassie liked her from the moment when, after Cassie had explained about her stalker, the deputy had sniffed and said, "Some of my male colleagues don't like admitting women sense things they don't."

"They don't because they don't have to be on guard as much," Cassie retorted.

"Exactly," Deputy Lindholm had said with a smile. It was while they were waiting for the crime-scene people to arrive that she asked, "You said Foxworth is in on this?"

"They're helping, yes," Cassie said. She glanced at him. "Jace brought them in." Then, sounding slightly anxious, she asked, "Is that a problem?"

"It never has been, that I know of. Opposite, in fact. One of our detectives, Brett Dunbar, swears by them. And we'd all pretty much swear by him, so..." She ended with a glance at Cutter. "The Foxworth dog? Heard about him, too."

Jace couldn't help smiling at that. Then, after he'd shown her where the car had been and given her the license number, she took some photos of the entry point. Then she went inside, taking care not to touch anything. The moment when he'd seen her draw her weapon had been the first time it had occurred to him—and to Cassie, judging by her quick intake of breath—that there might be somebody still inside.

"Cutter would have let us know, don't you think?" Cassie said, and Jace relaxed.

"Yes. Yes, he would." He was a little surprised at how certain he was of that, but the dog had proven uncannily clever so far, so there was no reason to think he'd fall down on the job now.

Shortly after Deputy Lindholm had come back out, assuring them the house was indeed empty, the crime-scene investigator arrived. Then there was more waiting while he processed the back door and the broken glass. Once he was done, the deputy gestured Cassie and Jace inside to see what had been taken or disturbed, cautioning them not to touch anything.

It wasn't long before Cassie was frowning. "I don't see anything missing. And it looks like he didn't touch a thing."

"Your desk," Jace said, and she turned to look at the corner of the living room that served as an office of sorts when she was home.

"It looks the same...except..."

"The flowers have been moved a bit, haven't they?"

"Yes," Cassie exclaimed, stepping over to look at the heavy glass vase that had been serving as a weight for a small stack of papers. "It's closer to the edge than it was."

Deputy Lindholm directed the man with the fingerprint kit to dust the glass vase.

"You're Grant's Flowers?" she asked then, looking at Cassie.

"Yes. It was my parents' business, and I run it now."

"Nice place. Bought my mom some Mother's Day flowers there this year, and they lasted forever."

Cassie looked pleased and distracted enough that Jace thought he could leave her for a moment. "I'll check the other rooms," he said. "No touching," he added when Deputy Lindholm glanced at him. She nodded, and he turned and headed toward the hallway.

His own room was simple—the only thing there was his pack in the closet, and it looked undisturbed. A glance in the adjacent bathroom showed it just as he'd left it this morning. Surely if the guy was looking for drugs or something, there'd be signs? Then again, maybe he was just careful.

He nudged open the door to Cassie's room, all the while bracing himself for the worst. If this guy had been after her in that way, if he'd been messing in her underwear drawer or something like that…

For a moment he just stood there, taking in the room he'd never really seen before. His first thought was relief; there was no sign of a crazed, fixated stalker. His second was gratitude; he wasn't sure how he would have handled seeing bras and panties strewn around. Cassie's, anyway.

Not the time, Cahill.

He made himself look for other signs. Instead he found himself noticing the room was very Cassie. Calm and organized, yet feminine in the small touches here and there. And tidy. That was the main thing. If the intruder had searched in here, he'd been inordinately careful about it.

He backed out, thinking even as he did so that this was likely as close as he was going to get to Cassidy Grant's bedroom.

With a grimace at himself for thinking about that now, he went toward the last door in the hallway, Cory's old room. He wasn't sure how you would tell if it had been searched, given all the crap the guy had stored in there, or if he would be able to see if anything had been disturbed, but—

The door wasn't closed all the way. And it had been, he was sure. He'd been the last one in there, to borrow those sweats.

Again not touching the doorknob, he nudged the door open with his foot. Or tried to; it jammed against something and he had to push with his knee.

"Damn."

The room had been cluttered before.

Now it was chaos.

Chapter 13

"I couldn't even begin to tell you if anything's missing," Cassidy said, feeling helpless. "I have no idea what all my brother stuffed in there."

"My question isn't so much what it is, but why do they think it's here?" Jace said.

"That, too," Cassidy said ruefully.

She had called May, who once she heard what had happened had immediately offered to stay over and keep the shop open. After that, feeling way out of her depth, all she could think of to do was make more coffee, so they were sitting at the kitchen counter with mugs full, discussing what had happened.

A soft woof from Cutter made Cassidy jump a little. Silly, she told herself, to be this on edge now, hours after it was all over. Besides, Cutter's quiet bark hadn't been one of warning.

Then there was a knock on the door. Jace got up immediately. She let him, because she was fighting the sense of invasion that had begun the moment she'd realized that man had been inside her home.

Jace came back with another man, tall, rangy, with short dark hair and a touch of gray at the temples that somehow only added to his good looks. Along with a serious expression, he wore dark slacks and a white dress shirt—sans tie, she noted—under a black topcoat with the collar turned up; it had started to rain again, judging by the beads of water she could see on the coat.

"Detective Brett Dunbar," Jace said. "He's the one the deputy mentioned."

Cassidy remembered Deputy Lindholm's words about him. She could see why; he had the air of a man who could be trusted utterly to do the right thing.

"Foxworth helps us out now and then, and vice versa," Dunbar said as he nodded at them both. And perhaps more importantly, Cutter greeted him as a friend, tail wagging happily. The man bent and scratched behind the dog's right ear with an easy familiarity. "And this guy...well, I owe him a great deal."

"Owe him?" Cassidy asked.

"If not for him, I'd never have met my wife."

Jace looked puzzled, then his eyes widened and he looked at Cutter. Dunbar nodded. Jace looked away. And she had absolutely no idea what all that had been about.

"Would you like some coffee?" she asked.

"Already at my limit, thanks," he said to her. "Sorry about your trouble. And doubly sorry that you weren't taken seriously before."

"I didn't have any real proof of anything," she said, to be fair. "Just a feeling."

The man smiled then, and Cassidy had the thought

that *good-looking* wasn't a strong enough term. "Thank you. Many don't see it that way."

Then he pulled a cell phone out of his coat pocket, tapped it a couple of times and set it down on the counter, where they could all see the photograph he'd called up.

The image resembled the man in prison, yet it was different. This man looked younger, smaller somehow. And his eyes…were lighter. As it all came together, Cassidy felt a sudden tightening in her midsection and a tingling chill, as if Dunbar had brought the cold rain in with him. Because some part of her knew this was the man who had been following her.

"Yes," she whispered.

"Frank Schiff," Dunbar said.

"Brother?" Jace guessed. "And not in prison?"

"Free as a bird," Dunbar said sourly. "Although he's building a record to match his brother's. Why I knew the name when I heard it."

"But I still don't understand why anyone like that would think I had something he wanted," Cassidy said, feeling more muddled than ever.

"But he doesn't," Jace said. She looked up at him. "It was Cory's room he searched."

She shook her head. "Cory would never be involved with people like this."

"Cassie, it doesn't matter whether or not you believe that Cory's involved. Just like it doesn't matter whether you know where whatever it is is."

"He's right," Dunbar said, and she saw him give Jace an approving look. "It only matters if he—" he nodded at the photo "—believes it."

She felt a renewed chill; she'd almost forgotten that aspect.

"When you went after him, was he carrying anything?" Dunbar said to Jace; he'd obviously been thoroughly briefed.

"Not in his hands. He used them both to go over the fence. Didn't see any bulges in his jacket pockets, either, but without knowing what he was looking for…" Jace ended with a shrug.

Dunbar nodded. "If it was something small, he still could have had it."

"But he was still inside, maybe still searching when we got here and Cutter sounded the alarm," Cassidy said, feeling like her brain was finally kicking into gear.

"Valid point," Dunbar agreed.

"But the most important thing is this proves he's not after Cassie herself, doesn't it?" Jace asked. She liked that that was most important to him and liked even more the tone in his voice that she couldn't quite put a name to. Protective, certainly, but more than that. Possessive, maybe, but not in a bad way. Whatever it was, his words made her feel a rush of relief.

"It would seem so," Dunbar agreed. The detective's brow furrowed, and his gaze seemed turned inward, as if he were trying to remember something. And then he snapped back to the present. "When was your brother last here?"

"About four months ago," Cassidy said.

Dunbar nodded. "Give me a minute." He picked up the phone and walked out into the living room. When he came back, his expression was grim enough that Cassidy felt a stab of dread.

"Buddy of mine in Seattle," he said, explaining the phone call. "Seems the criminal enterprise that landed Frank's brother in prison had a little problem a while back. Somebody stole a chunk of their stolen money."

"That seems fair," Jace said drily.

Dunbar flashed a potent grin this time. "Does, doesn't it?"

"How big a chunk?" Cassidy asked.

"Healthy six figures big."

Jace whistled at that. And cut it off abruptly. "Wait. How long ago?" Dunbar only looked at him and nodded, again almost approvingly. "Damn," Jace said.

Cassidy looked from one to the other, bewildered. "What?"

Dunbar shifted his gaze to her. "The money was stolen a little over four months ago."

It still took her a moment. But when she got there she felt a wave of nausea sweep over her.

Four months ago.

The last time Cory had been here.

"No," Cassie said flatly.

"He's right, you'd be safer," Jace said.

It was Rafe who, after everyone had finally cleared out, had made the suggestion of Cassie temporarily decamping to a hotel. There weren't a lot of options here, but there was one at the casino not too far away. Rafe had originally suggested they both go, but Jace had recoiled at the thought, wondering how many nights his father had spent in the place while piling up that crippling debt he had left for his family to deal with.

"Foxworth will cover it," Rafe had said. "And we've got friends on their security team."

"Seems you have friends everywhere," Jace had said.

"Yes," Rafe had answered simply.

But Cassie had been as determined as he was not to go, although for different reasons. She had politely declined to Rafe, but now that they were alone, she'd let out a bit of her true feelings. She was pacing like a caged tiger, and he had the uneasy feeling she could be just as snarly if she let it all loose.

"So I go sit and wait for you to fix this? No, thank you. I'll be safe when this is over. Until then, I'm in."

He sat down, feeling suddenly weary. "Maybe it is over. Maybe he finished his search. Maybe he knows now whatever it is wasn't in that room."

"And you think that would end it?"

He didn't, not really, but he didn't want to voice even in his mind what could come next if their burglar really had finished his search. The guy could really come after Cassie, thinking she knew, that Cory had told her something.

"No," he admitted.

Cory. Damn it, how could he do this? How could he let himself get in so deep it put his own sister in danger? Because he was certain down deep that Cory was somehow at the center of this.

"Let him come back," Cassie said stubbornly. "We'll catch him this time. Third time's the charm and all that."

Jace whirled on her then. "So that's it? You want to be bait?"

"Of course I don't. But I'm the only bait we have."

He stared at her for a long moment. Then he let out a long breath. "You always did have more will and nerve than Cory ever did."

Pain flared in her eyes, and he was sorry he'd mentioned the name. He was sorry about a lot of things. And reeling a bit inside, from having gone from the hot, fierce sweetness of that kiss outside to this harsh reminder of a very real threat.

"You knew," she said. It sounded like an accusation.

"I knew...what?"

"Was Cory always this deep into trouble and I didn't see it, or did he get worse?" He grimaced. Tried a shrug as answer. She wasn't buying. "He's your best friend. You have to know things I don't."

"I told you, haven't seen him in years."

She abruptly stopped pacing. Turned to look at him. And when she spoke, the edge in her voice had softened. "And yet you came when I called anyway."

"Of course. I—"

"Promised. I know." She drew in a deep breath. "And you always had twice the honor and integrity my brother ever had."

He opened his mouth. Shut it again, wanting those words, spoken by her, to hang in the air until they soaked into his mind forever. Because they made him feel as if he'd been given a medal or something. If Cassie Grant thought that of him, then maybe the battle really had been worth it.

"I knew that," she went on after a moment when he didn't speak. "I knew you were…a better person. So I guess on some level I knew he was…"

"I'm sorry, Cassie."

It was all he could think of to say. Driven by a need he knew he couldn't beat down at the moment, he stood up, walked over to her and put his arms around her. She went still for an instant but then softened into his embrace, leaning into him as if he were the only thing keeping her upright.

"How bad was it?" she asked after a moment. "How much did he hide from me? How much don't I know about my own brother?"

"A bit," he said.

"Tell me. I need to know, Jace."

He sighed. "What am I supposed to tell you when I haven't seen him in four years?"

"What's the worst thing he did?"

"Depends who you ask."

"Don't dodge anymore, Jace. Please."

"The worst thing that I know of? Stole a car."

Cassie went still. "What?" He only shrugged. She pulled back. He missed the feel of her instantly. But he could almost hear that mind of hers clicking into gear. "He never got arrested."

"He nearly did. Saw a cop and freaked, took the car back."

"When?"

"Junior year of high school."

She looked suddenly thoughtful. "I remember…

him arguing with my dad, around then, because they wouldn't buy him one."

"He was ticked because your parents wanted him to work and pay for at least half of it."

Cassie looked at him consideringly, and he could almost see her putting things together. "That must sound ridiculous to you," she said softly.

"Pretty much," he agreed.

"You weren't…with him."

"That didn't sound like a question."

"It wasn't." She gave him a faint smile. "I know you weren't. You wouldn't. That integrity thing."

For a moment he let the warmth well up in him again. Her respect meant more to him than he ever would have guessed.

Then she sighed. "But apparently he went on to… bigger and worse things."

"Apparently."

"When you saw him last…he was asking for money?" He nodded. "Why?"

"Said he owed some guys."

"If you didn't say, 'Get a job,' I admire your restraint."

She said it so sourly it both startled him and made him laugh. "Look, I know this isn't easy. He's your brother and it must be hard to…"

"Admit he's a complete flake? Yes."

She was handling this well. But then, he should have known she would. "Kind of weird."

"What?"

"That you two turned out so…differently."

Her mouth twisted wryly. "I thought it was our parents dying that made him go a little off the rails. But obviously he was screwed up well before that."

"He was just always looking for the easy way," Jace said. "Which also probably explains why you so rarely saw him."

Her brow furrowed. "What do you mean?"

"He probably found it hard to face you. He's wrecked his life, and you've taken what your parents left and made a good one."

She looked troubled at first, but then she smiled at him. "I'd say you're the expert on taking what you're left and making good on it."

He wasn't sure when her high regard had become crucial to him, but clearly it had. And he was still basking in the warmth of it when she spoke again.

"So. Shall we venture into the wasteland of Cory's old room and see if we can find what we hope that guy didn't?"

"You sure you're ready to tackle that?"

"It's what comes next, isn't it?"

She turned to head for the hallway. And Jace had the thought that despite their very dissimilar lives so far, perhaps they weren't so different after all.

Chapter 14

"Seriously?" Jace said.

Cassidy turned to look at him. He was holding up something limp and a muddy shade of brown. It took her a moment to realize it was a totally deflated football.

"Maybe he wanted to use it again someday?"

"Don't think so," Jace said, turning it so she could see the rip along one seam that made the thing useless.

She sighed. "He didn't hide something in it, did he?"

Jace looked startled for an instant, but then his expression shifted. "I'm sorry, Cassie."

"For what? Agreeing to search this mess?"

"No. That you have to think that way."

"Oh. Yeah. Well." She gestured around at the piles of stuff they'd been slowly sorting through. "Keeping my mind occupied with this helps."

She'd decided that she'd had enough of being her brother's free junk room, and anything without any clear usefulness would go. Jace added the ruined ball to the trash bag in the hall that was rapidly filling. After, she noted, he had pulled the gap open and peered inside.

"Do you wonder if we'll throw away what he was looking for because we don't know what it is?" she asked.

"Yes," he said. "But I figure hang on to it all until they catch the guy."

She nodded. "Good idea. Assuming he'll talk," she added.

Jace came back into the room, stepping over a pile of old shoes. "I don't know," he said with an upward quirk of one corner of his mouth, "I'm thinking that Detective Dunbar would be pretty good at getting people to talk."

She smiled at that. "Me, too."

She picked up a book from the pile on the small desk and flipped through it, looking for notes slipped between the pages or writing on the pages. Finding nothing, she set it on the small stack. She had been the reader, not Cory, so there weren't that many to check.

"This Foxworth is really something," she said for something to say.

"Yes. And he—" he gestured to the hallway where Cutter was plopped, watching them work with apparent interest "—is the strangest of all."

The dog's head came up. "Aw, did he call you strange, boy?" she called out to him teasingly.

Jace laughed and turned to stuff a pair of jeans into the trash bag. For a moment she just stood there, torn between savoring that laugh and loving to watch the way he moved.

"Rafe said he's only the front man on this because the rest of Foxworth is off at various places for the Thanksgiving break," he said idly as he tackled a shirt Cassidy didn't think she'd ever seen her brother wearing.

"But he is not?"

"I got the feeling he prefers it that way."

She put down the last book. "What about you? Thanksgiving, I mean. You'll need to get back to your mom's."

He shrugged—again—without looking at her. "She knows this might go past."

Another week of living like this? She wasn't sure she could handle that. And not, she admitted to herself, just because of whatever threat Cory had brought down on her, but because the more time she spent with Jace, the more she wanted to spend.

And that's not all you want.

That little voice in her head was becoming more and more adamant. At least she was consistent, she told herself. Everything that had attracted her to Jace ten years ago still did. Only now there was so much more to it. He'd proven himself to be everything she'd thought him then, and more. Much more.

It was crazy, she thought. Cory had had the best parents around, and he'd gone haywire. Jace had had none of that, and he'd come out this man full of integrity.

They were the only reason I ever knew my father's way was wrong.

His words, whispered in that harsh, tight voice, echoed in her head.

"What?"

His voice snapped her out of her thoughts, and she

realized he'd noticed she'd been staring at him. She grabbed at the first thing that popped into her mind.

"If this isn't over by then, what shall we do on Thanksgiving?"

He went very still. Too still. She played back what she'd said in her mind. Was it the *we* that had frozen him in place? She'd only meant that he was staying here, so of course he'd be here, and by *we* she only meant that... but it sounded like it was the other kind of *we*, like they were a unit, a couple.

"I...hadn't thought about it."

That was all he said, and just when the silence started feeling awkward, Cutter got to his feet. He worked his way into the room by hopping over the trash bag and threading himself agilely through the piles. He paused to sniff as he went, and Cassidy wondered when he stopped a couple of times for a particularly long sniff if he'd found the burglar's scent.

As if he'd had the same thought, Jace began to follow the dog, looking at the places where he'd stopped for a longer inspection. But then the animal reached the pile of clothes Jace had pulled out of the closet all at once to go through one at a time. He stopped and began to paw at the pile.

"You smell something, buddy?" Jace asked softly.

He began to pick up the items of clothing one by one, discarding them as the dog kept pawing. When he reached a dark green leather jacket and picked it up, the dog quit pawing and sat down.

"This what you were after, dog?"

"That's my jacket!" Cassidy exclaimed. "I've been

looking for that. I thought I'd left it somewhere. Did he just smell it was mine?"

"Maybe."

"And why on earth did Cory have it in his closet?" She threaded her way through other piles and took the classic blazer-cut soft leather garment.

"I'm wondering when."

"When I lost it?" She drew back slightly, thinking. "I wore it to May's birthday dinner, and that was the last time I saw it. It's my favorite, so I went back to the restaurant twice hoping they'd found it. Thank you, kind sir." She bent and stroked Cutter's head. The dog looked steadily at her, as if he were trying to communicate something more about his discovery.

"When was that?" Jace asked.

"That was—" She stopped.

"Four months ago?" Jace suggested, gently.

"Cory was here when I got home," she said, her voice sounding hollow even to herself. She stared down at the jacket. "But why?"

"Not something he'd mistake for his," Jace said. She thought his voice sounded a little too neutral. As if he'd already reached a conclusion and was just waiting, Jace-like, for her to get there.

"No. So it had to be intentional."

She looked down at the jacket again. The leather was buttery soft against her fingers. She remembered how she'd torn her closet apart looking for it, since about half her wardrobe was built around it. But she had treasured it for more than that. It had been a gift from her parents, chosen by her mother because it brought out the green in her hazel eyes.

"But why?" she repeated blankly. "Why would he take this, when he knew it was my favorite jacket, knew what it meant to me because Mom and Dad gave it to me? I've been heartbroken over losing it."

"Maybe because he knew you'd keep looking for it," Jace said.

"And eventually find it in here?" She looked around at the mess. "I probably would have cleared this out at some point, but it never would have occurred to me to look in here for it. And again, why? Unless it was some kind of stupid game he was playing…"

"He did have the tendency."

"But to what end?" She was feeling bewildered now.

"Maybe because if you ever did tackle this room, the jacket would jump out at you as…out of place."

"And?"

He gave that half shrug she was beginning to dislike. "Anything in the pockets?"

"You mean like a note or something?" Quickly she checked but came up only with a piece of metal tucked into the single inside pocket. She pulled it out, and with it came a small piece of an evergreen branch she must have picked up somewhere. She stared at the object, puzzled in a different way now.

Jace reached out and took the four-inch-long piece that appeared to be coated with red plastic down to the end, which had an angular hole it in. "Looks like a valve shutoff lever."

"Yes. But I never put that there. I never used that

inside pocket, and I never had reason to carry around a…shutoff lever."

"So I guess the question is why would Cory stick the thing in there?"

Cassidy shook her head. "I have no idea."

He grimaced. "Neither do I. Other than it would be puzzling to you. Make you wonder."

"I'm going to call him again," she said decisively. "Maybe this is all some Cory game, and now that I've finally found this, he'll call me back."

"He always had a game plan," Jace said, again in that neutral tone.

She didn't bother to point out that her brother's plans rarely worked out as he expected. Because she knew Jace already knew that.

"Aren't you tired of pacing?"

She was making him tired. And apparently worrying Cutter, because the dog kept walking over to her and nudging her hand. At the moment he'd given up and come over to sit beside Jace.

"Worried," she explained succinctly.

"Cory," he said.

She didn't deny it. "Shouldn't I be? With him not calling back and now his cell number's out of service?"

"Maybe he couldn't pay the bill," Jace said.

She stopped, turned to look at him. He waited for her to say something pitying about him having been in those circumstances. Which he had been.

"Maybe." She stopped there. But a moment later, as if she'd known exactly where his mind had been, she said softly, "It must feel good, to have proven your father wrong a hundred times over."

He wished she hadn't gone there; he didn't like thinking about it, let alone talking about it. "I just did what had to be done," he said. "He's not my motivation, not anymore."

She turned to look at him then. "Good. He's not worth even that much thought."

She said it fiercely. And that made him smile. "If he ever shows up again, I'll send him to you."

"Good," she repeated. "I'd like to tell him a thing or two."

Then she frowned. She started toward him, and in the same moment, Cutter rose and hopped up onto the end of the couch. He saw the briefest hesitation as she gave the dog an odd look, but then she continued and took the only space the dog had left her. Right beside him. He didn't know whether to thank the dog or snap at him. Cutter merely looked at him, his expression... smug.

"Do you think he ever will show up?"

He shifted his gaze back to her. "Only if I strike it rich."

Her expression was as sour as his tone had been. "Or win the lottery."

He let out a snort of laughter. "That was his game. He always said, 'Somebody's gotta win.'"

"I almost wish you would, so you could tell him exactly where to go."

"Have to buy a ticket first, and that isn't going to happen."

There would be no gambling for him, of any kind.

He'd always, deep down, wondered if there was some need to risk everything that could be passed on. He didn't care to find out the hard way.

"You'd never be like him, Jace. Ever."

He blinked. She'd always been pretty good at guessing what he was thinking, but this was getting...

He wasn't sure what it was getting. He'd been going to finish that with *scary*, but that wasn't at all a word he'd use in connection with Cassie.

"I used to buy a ticket now and then," she said. "Think about what I'd do if I won big."

"What would you do?" He was genuinely curious.

"Quit working six days a week just to stay even, that's for sure. Sometimes I'd like to just walk away." She stopped suddenly, giving him a guilt-stricken look. "Listen to me whining, when you—"

"Don't worry about me."

Her expression changed as she looked at him, went from guilty to something much softer. "Sorry," she said. "Not possible."

And suddenly all he could think of was that kiss. He scrambled for something to say. Anything to say. "How bad is it? With the shop?"

She sighed. "There's a lot of competition, and our internet sales aren't where I'd like them to be, but a website redesign is a project I haven't had time for. But it's not as bad as it would be if my parents hadn't left us the house free and clear." She glanced around. "It's kind of...unsettling, though. To think that they inherited this house from Dad's parents because they died in a plane crash, and then we inherit it from them for the same reason."

"Have you thought of selling it? For the cash infusion?"

"Yes." She looked slightly embarrassed. "I know, it's silly, but I couldn't decide which was worse, living here in this house where everything reminds me, or selling it when it's been in the family for three generations now."

"That's not silly," he said. "It's...something not many people have anymore."

"It's a lot nicer than my tiny little apartment in Seattle, that's for sure. Talk about needing a cash infusion."

He looked at her curiously. "You lived in Seattle?"

"For a while. School."

"You did go to U-Dub, then," he said, using the shortened local nickname for the University of Washington.

"For a while," she said. Her tone was just a little too neutral. Then the math hit him. She'd gone until her parents had been killed.

"I'm sorry. That you didn't get to finish."

"I'm not. I found I didn't miss it much. Was glad to be out of some of it, in fact. Besides, there was the shop to take over."

"Was Cory there for you, at all?"

"He came home," she said. "He was in Portland at the time, doing what I never found out."

Because he hadn't wanted her to know? There was certainly enough trouble for Cory to get into in Portland. He hesitated, then decided to risk asking, "Why did he come home four months ago?"

He saw her glance flick toward the coffee table and

the small lever they'd found in her jacket pocket. "He said he wanted to see me."

"You don't sound convinced."

"I wasn't. He said that, but we spent exactly one afternoon together. The rest of the time he was gone."

"Where?"

"Visiting friends, he said."

"Did he say anything? In that one afternoon?"

She sighed. "I've gone over and over it in my head, but I can't think of anything that would explain...that." She ended with a gesture at the lever.

"He was obviously trying to say something."

"Somehow I doubt he was referring to Archimedes, which is the only thing that brings to mind."

"'Give me a lever long enough'? No, Cory doesn't seem the type."

And suddenly they were staring at each other, and he knew they were both thinking of the day long ago when she had been assigned an essay on that famous quote. At thirteen she'd been a bit iffy on the concept, and fifteen-year-old Jace had used a rock, a board and Cory's basketball to demonstrate. And when she'd understood but hadn't seen how you could possibly have a lever long enough to actually move the earth, he'd been the one to suggest to her that, given the essay was for an English class and not physics, her teacher might be asking for something a little less literal.

"I always adored you," she said quietly, "but I didn't realize until much later in life just how special you were. Not many would take that kind of time to help out a friend's little sister with that kind of thing."

He swallowed at her first words, and it was surprisingly hard to get words past the lump in his throat. "It was easier than the roof jump."

She laughed at that, but then her expression changed yet again. She had always been such a live wire, jumping from thought to idea and back again so quickly it became a sort of game for him to try to keep up. "I finally confessed to my dad about that. Much later."

"You did?"

That surprised him, because her greatest fear in that moment was that her father would find out she'd disobeyed him about climbing up there. Jumping from the branch of the big maple tree to the roof had been one thing, but going the other way, from the solid roof to the much less substantial branch, had been something else again.

"Yes. And when I told him he was right, that I was scared to go back down the way I got up, he asked how I did it."

He went still. "Did you tell him?"

"Of course. No point in confessing unless you're going to come clean, is there?"

He had no answer for that. A confession like that to his father would have likely ended up with him confined to his room for the rest of the year. With a screaming lecture every day of it to remind him of why he wasn't worth the food he ate.

"What did he say?" he managed to ask.

"That he was glad I'd insisted you catch me, not Cory." Jace blinked. "What?"

"That my brother might dodge away at the last minute if he thought he was going to get hurt, but if you said you'd do it, you'd do it."

He had no words for how it made him feel, that the man he'd admired so much—in fact, had so often wished was his own father—had had such faith in him. It made his feelings about his real father even worse, but somehow they mattered less. He lowered his gaze, picked at a loose thread on his worn jeans. The silence spun out, and she let it. She'd chattered endlessly, animatedly back then. But now she had learned the power of silence, the pressure it could apply. And after a long moment, he broke.

"When I... When things got really bad at home, I used to tell myself I'd never be like him. But I needed somebody I did want to be like, when I grew up. Somebody to...emulate, I guess. Your father was it."

She moved so quickly he didn't realize what she was doing until she'd thrown her arms around him. "Oh, Jace, there's no better tribute you could give him. He would be thrilled. And honored."

He didn't mean to do it. If he'd taken a half second to think, he wouldn't have. But she was right there, looking up at him with those green-gold eyes, that sweet, soft mouth so close, and he couldn't stop himself.

He lowered his head. Slowly, giving her every chance to pull away. Instead she tilted her head back and slipped a hand around the back of his neck. And at the first touch of her lips on his, nothing else mattered.

Chapter 15

Cassidy had wondered if what happened when they kissed before had just been the built-up want of the twenty-two years since she'd first laid eyes on him at the tender age of five. Even then he'd stood out to her, seeming so much older than her brother, even though they were both seven. And she'd adored him with all the fervor her child's heart could muster.

That had only increased over the decade he'd lived—or rather, survived—down the street. Other girls had fantasized about the latest young phenom, but she had always found something wrong with whoever the flavor of the moment was. But in that heart she always knew what was really wrong with them was they weren't Jace. But she kept that part secret, not wanting the teasing that would inevitably occur if she betrayed her feelings for someone real, someone they could see and giggle at. And then she'd come home from school one day, late because she'd been chattering with those friends, and her mother told her she'd just missed Jace when he'd come to say goodbye.

She'd been heartbroken then. Now…now he was here, in her arms, searing her to her very soul with a kiss that blasted every question she had out of her heart and mind. He was kissing her as if he felt the same way, that the answer to everything was here, now, in this kiss. Could it even happen like this if it didn't go both ways?

She shivered as he traced the line of her lips with his tongue. Yes, yes, this was the feel, the taste she had longed for all her life. She touched his tongue with the tip of her own and felt the jolt that went through him as if it were a continuation of the one that had shot through her. And when he deepened the kiss, making it no less than a claiming of her mouth, the utter rightness of it flooded her.

She needed him closer, ever closer, and in the instant she thought it, he shifted her back onto the couch from which Cutter had mysteriously vanished. She pulled him with her, suddenly craving the weight of him on her as she'd never craved anything in her life. She wanted his hands on her, hers on him—she wanted to explore every inch of him. Even as she thought it, she became aware of several urgent inches of him as he pressed against her.

He broke the kiss, and she took what felt like her first breath since his mouth had come down on hers. "Cassie…"

She felt another shiver down her spine at the rough, low sound of her name, that name that had always been reserved only for him. It was followed by a rush of heat unlike anything she'd ever felt, and the collision of the two opposing sensations had her practically shaking.

"Jace, I—"

She stopped and Jace groaned aloud at the sound of the buzz from both of their Foxworth phones. Hers was in the kitchen and his right here on the table, so he reached out and touched the red button. Still on top of her, as if he hoped to resume where they'd left off as soon as possible. Which was exactly what she wanted, and she slid her hands to his hips to hold him there in case he'd had any ideas about moving.

"Yeah?" His voice was more than a little gruff.

"Interrupt something?" Rafe's voice was unmistakably amused.

Jace glanced back at her, his expression clearly saying, "If you only knew."

"Sorry," Rafe said, not waiting for an actual answer, "but I need to ask Cassidy something."

"I'm here," she said, smothering a little cry of protest when Jace lifted himself and sat up.

"When exactly did you last talk to your brother?"

She pulled herself upright on the couch, putting her feet back on the floor in more ways than one. It took her a moment to clear her head. Jace Cahill was a very potent brew. "I... Five...no, six weeks ago. Around the first of October."

"Do you know where he was then?"

"He said he was in Salt Lake City. But that he was leaving the next day for Las Vegas."

There was a moment of silence. Then Rafe said, "I have to send you a photo."

Just the fact that he sounded reluctant made Cassidy's stomach clench. Instinctively she hunched over, as if she could protect herself from whatever blow the Foxworth man was about to deliver. And then she felt the warmth of Jace's arm around her as they looked at the phone, and it gave her strength.

"Is he dead?" she asked bluntly, thinking the worst and that this photo would be of his body.

"No," Rafe said quickly. "Not that I know. Sorry, should have said that first." He sounded irritated at himself. And it made her think of what he'd said that first day. *I'm not usually the front man for Foxworth.*

The photo came through, and she immediately saw the reason for his hesitation. It was a mug shot, with the label "St. George Police Department," and a date—a week after he'd called her—beneath the face. The face that was unmistakably her brother's. Nausea welled up inside her.

"Utah? Guess he didn't quite make it to Vegas," Jace said, not a trace of shock or surprise in his voice. It made her wonder what he else he knew about Cory that he hadn't told her.

"What for?" She was surprised at how even her voice was.

"Shoplifting from a convenience store."

"Is he in jail?"

"No. He swore he just forgot to pay when he got a phone call, and the store agreed to accept restitution, so the charges were dropped."

"You mean…he had the money?"

"Apparently."

She shook her head slowly, baffled. "Then why…?"

"For the kick," Jace said flatly. "Cory always wanted

to test the limits, see what he could get away with." She turned to look at him. He shrugged. "Your parents kept him in line at home, but outside…he was always testing the limits."

"We don't know yet where he is now, but we're on it. I'll get back to you when I've got anything more," Rafe said. Then added, again as if he wasn't used to the niceties, "Sorry to hit you with that."

"Not your fault," Cassidy said. And for a moment after the call had ended she sat wondering just whose fault it was.

She was pacing again. Jace could almost see what she was thinking. He stood up, crossed to stand in front of her. "Stop. Cory made his own choices. He always did."

Yes, he did. Including not answering her calls, when clearly he still had his phone and it worked. Unless he'd lied to the police about that.

Cassie turned to look at Jace straight on. "How did you stay best friends with him without getting sucked into that stuff?"

He drew in a breath, slightly uncomfortable. "I did, a couple of times, in the beginning. And we got away with a couple of things. But I'd come home and look at my mom, who was putting up with so much, and I just…couldn't."

"And your father?"

His mouth twisted. "That, too. I was afraid if I got arrested that'd tip him over the edge."

"Would you do something for me?"

The way she was looking at him right now, he'd have

said yes to anything. And that thought sent his mind careening out of control, back to those moments on the couch, when he'd had her sweet body beneath him and her mouth on his.

Make love to you? Have hot, wild, slamming sex with you? Or scariest of all, both at once?

"What?" he managed to get out.

"Help me not think about Cory and all this for a while?"

He swallowed. She wanted comforting, he told himself. That's all. He reined his mind in. Tried the same with his body, with less success. A sudden memory shot through his mind, he wasn't sure why, of the day she'd jumped from the roof of this house. He remembered grinning at her, as much to keep her from being scared at what she'd done than anything.

You did it!

I knew you'd catch me.

He felt a sudden, warm pressure at the back of his legs. Cutter, leaning into him. Pushing him. Toward Cassie. As if the dog knew what was needed and was tired of waiting for him to figure it out.

I knew you'd catch me.

That's what she needed. She needed someone, in the midst of all this, to catch her.

Cutter nudged again. Jace gave in. He crossed the two feet between them in a single step. He knew it had been the right thing when she slipped her arms around him and tightened them, as if she wanted him closer. He closed his eyes, allowing himself just this moment, even as he warned himself again it was comfort she wanted.

Her world had been upended already, and her realization about her brother had no doubt shaken her to the core.

But he couldn't stop his instant response to her closeness, her softness, her heat.

Just because she had a crush on you years ago doesn't mean she really wants you now. She just needs someone to hang on to right now, that's all. It's Cassie—she's like a sister to you.

But she'd kissed him. Hot and sweet and deep, she'd kissed him. She'd been with him all the way, he couldn't deny that.

But that was before she'd had to sit there and look at a mug shot of her brother.

She pressed herself even closer to him until he realized she couldn't help but notice the effect she was having on him. Again. His jaw tightened. He tried to think, but it was getting more difficult with every breath, every moment she simply stayed in his arms, searing him in ways she couldn't even realize.

"Cassie," he said, and it came out a low, rough sound.

"Yes," she answered, and his pulse slammed into overdrive.

She didn't mean it that way. She was just answering. She didn't mean yes to you.

Yes to sex with you, he amended with the tiny bit of reason that was still functioning, because that's where this was headed. And his body screamed at him that she'd meant exactly that while his reeling mind tried to say she was in no mental condition right now to make that decision. And he spared a smothered oath for Rafe's timing. *Interrupt something?* Oh, yeah.

With one of the greatest efforts of his life, he tamped down the heat. Ignored the body that didn't want to be slowed.

"We—"

She had turned her head, pressed her lips to his throat. His own groan stopped his words. He couldn't help himself—he closed his eyes and let his head loll back, savoring the feel of her mouth on his skin, even knowing that if he let this go on another minute, stopping was going to kill him.

But he had to.

"Cassie. Stop."

"Why?" She sounded genuinely puzzled.

"So many reasons."

"Such as?"

He gathered what breath he could get. Lifted his head and looked at her. "I…don't have anything. Protection."

"I do." He blinked, surprised. "May," she said. "She's ever hopeful on my behalf. Next reason?"

"Because you're…off balance right now. Your life's gone crazy on you."

She tilted her head back. "Noble," she said.

He blinked. "What?"

"I forgot to add nobility along with honor and integrity."

He swore under his breath. "I'm on the edge here, Cassie."

"Which way do I push?" He stared at her. "To send you over the edge," she explained, as if to be sure he understood.

"You don't want this. Me." Okay, he'd finally gone

crazy. She was standing here, offering him what he'd been hot for practically since she'd opened the door when he'd first arrived. And he was trying to talk her out of it?

"I have wanted you," she said, enunciating the words as if she wanted to be absolutely certain they were clear, "since the first day I saw you. The ways changed as I grew up, but never the wanting."

"I've only been here three days. You're not one for some convenient fling." Yes, crazy. It was the only explanation. "And I can't offer you anything—"

"But yourself? That's what I'm asking for, Jace. The guy who does what's right and keeps his promises. That's what's important to me."

That did it. He was done fighting this. He had the feeling he never would have won anyway. Not against a determined Cassidy Grant.

And especially not when he didn't really want to win.

Never, as a child or as a young woman who at least understood the basics, had she ever imagined anything like this. She'd yearned for this, for Jace, for so long that she'd expected finally having him in her arms, touching him, kissing him, would be wonderful.

She'd never expected it to be so searingly soul-deep.

From the first moment she'd slid her hands under the hem of his shirt, felt her fingertips slide over his skin, felt the taut muscle beneath, the heat she'd felt before began to build until it was nearly unbearable. No matter how much she touched, she wanted more. The image of that day he'd been wearing only the borrowed sweats, riding low on his hips, shot through her mind. She wanted…no, needed to see that broad, strong chest again. Needed to see, and touch.

And suddenly she was so intent on ridding him of that shirt that she barely noticed his hands had moved until the moment he grabbed the hem of her own shirt and pulled it off her, then shed his own himself. She nearly gasped at the sight, the feel of him as she stroked that chest, down to his ridged abdomen. And then his hands did the opposite to her, sliding up her ribs to cup her breasts, and she did gasp at the blast of heat that went through her.

Suddenly every bit of clothing between them was something that had to be gotten rid of. Now. She wanted to feel him, all of him, skin to skin, and she couldn't wait another second for it. He had turned calm, logical Cassidy Grant into a wild, desperate thing she didn't even recognize. His urgency as he tugged away the rest of her clothes only fed her own.

She moaned as she got her wish—he pulled her against him, and she felt the heat of him from knees to shoulders. Felt the hardness of him pressing against her belly, making the ache low and deep inside her almost unbearable. Then he was kissing her again, deeply, fiercely, and she thought she couldn't stand another moment.

The instant she thought it he swept her up, still kissing her hungrily as he cradled her against his chest. Then he pulled back, breaking the kiss, and she nearly whimpered at the loss. She felt him draw in a deep breath, as if he were humming inside as much as she was.

"Cassie," he whispered. "You're sure? Absolutely sure?"

"As sure as that day I jumped off the roof," she said.

For an instant he looked startled, then a slow, warm smile curved his mouth. That wonderful, tempting mouth she wanted on hers again. She wanted that mouth everywhere.

"My bed's bigger," she suggested.

"We might need the room," he answered fervently.

And then they were there, naked, entwined, and she had had enough of waiting. And she realized that understanding the basics was far, far different from knowing what this would be like. She'd waited for this man practically her entire life, even when she hadn't understood what it all meant. And now she was done with waiting. She ran her hands over him eagerly, savoring every little sign of answering response, a groan here, a catch in his breath there and the convulsive jerk of his body when her hands swept lower and caressed his swollen flesh.

"Careful," he said in a voice she could only call a low growl. "I'm trying to go slow, but it's been a long time."

"Why," she said, stroking him, savoring the feel of impossibly silken skin over erect flesh that made her shiver in anticipation, "would you want to even try to go slow?"

"Because you deserve—"

"This?" she asked, rubbing her thumb over the tip until he shuddered. "I certainly hope so."

That quickly he rolled her beneath him, and she shuddered in turn at the glorious feel of his weight on her. *This*, she thought. This was what it was all about, this was what it was supposed to be, what she'd never felt before. Because her heart had been given long ago, the first time she'd looked into those blue eyes and fallen into their depths. The first time he'd smiled at her, when he had so little to smile about in his life.

He slid his hand down between them and stroked her with a tentative finger. She felt her own readiness in the slickness he found, and in the involuntary arching of her hips upward to his touch.

"Slow next time," he muttered.

"And the time after that," she agreed.

And then he was sliding into her inch by inch, stretching her, filling the place that seemed made for him. She heard him let out a low oath as she stretched to accommodate him. She moaned again as the emptiness vanished and she felt whole, as if what had ever been missing was now as it should be.

For a moment he froze, as if he were afraid to move. She closed her eyes, focusing utterly on the feel of him inside her, wanting to have the memory of this first time forever. But her body had other ideas, and it was only seconds before she lifted involuntarily in invitation.

It was clearly all Jace needed, for he began to move. His first withdrawal nearly made her cry out at the loss, but then he drove back in and took her breath away.

"Yes," she whispered, clutching at him, lifting to take him in to the hilt. "Yes, yes."

Again he drew back and plunged forward, and she arched upward to meet him, her body already on the edge of flight. She could feel it, was amazed at it, the speed of it. But she had been waiting for this, for him, for a very long time.

That was her last coherent thought, for when he thrust again her entire body clenched, and wave after wave of a pleasure she'd never known reduced her to helpless moans.

And then she felt him go rigid against her, and he cried out her name and shuddered in her arms.

It had been worth the wait.

Jace awoke slowly and slightly disoriented. Not a surprise, he thought, given the crazy dream—

No. There was nothing dreamlike about the warmth curled up at his back, even tucked behind his knees. Nothing dreamlike about the feel of silken skin against his. Nothing dreamlike about the faint, sweet scent wafting off the flowers on the nightstand.

Cassie's room. Cassie's bed. With Cassie in it.

Heat erupted in him, pouring like molten lava along every nerve. It had really happened. That incredible, unbelievable night had really happened. And as it ran through his mind, the first, impossibly sweet time—so quick it would have been embarrassing if not for the fact that Cassie had climaxed at his third stroke, ending it for him with the fierce clenching of her body—and all the other times after that, when his body had overridden the mind telling him to let her sleep, when she in turn had awakened him and it had ended up with her riding him so sensuously it had taken everything he had to hold back until he felt her body tighten again and she cried out his name in that tone of wonder he knew he'd carry with him to his grave.

He kept his eyes closed, knowing as soon as he opened them he was going to have to deal with reality. She stirred behind him, snuggling even closer. At least in sleep, she had no regrets. He wasn't sure how anyone could regret a night like last night, but…he wasn't the one who'd slept with a guy who had literally no prospects, who was essentially starting over at twenty-nine.

I have wanted you since the first day I saw you…

Well, she'd surely had him. The question was, how was she going to feel when she woke up? Was it going to be one of those awkward mornings after? He tried to imagine Cassie being one of those cool, casual women who moved on without a second thought. The picture wouldn't even form. No, she'd expect…something. And he had no idea what. He had nothing to give, anyway.

He had to smother a rueful laugh; had he thought she'd be the one with regrets?

At an odd, unexpected touch, his eyes snapped open. Cutter sat beside the bed, one foot gently pawing at the comforter. Not urgently, and without a sound, so he gathered it wasn't a warning.

"You need out, boy?" he asked softly.

The dog stood up in answer. Clear enough, Jace thought.

He slid out of bed, missing Cassie's warmth the instant his skin felt the chill in the room. A glance at her Foxworth phone, that had ended up on his nightstand, told him it was nearly seven. Still before sunrise here this time of year, the sky not getting lighter as much as the darkness lessening. Still, it was later than he'd slept in a very long time.

He went out to the living room, found his jeans on the floor and tugged them on. Grinning—and heating up—at the memory of Cassie tugging them off him. It wasn't until he grabbed up his shirt and socks and was headed for his boots that he realized what he'd thought. *His nightstand.*

Like he had some genuine claim here, like by taking her, the sweet fire she'd offered, he'd taken the rest, too. He felt a sudden burst of yearning for it to be true, for her life to open to include him for more than just the duration of…whatever this was.

He shut down the thought, the wish, with the long experience of one who knew too well how useless wishing was. Cutter waited politely at the door while he finished dressing. He took a moment to scribble a note to Cassie and left it on the kitchen counter by the coffee-maker. If she woke while they were gone, she'd probably head straight there and see it. If she didn't…well, maybe he'd just slide right back into bed with her for a morning hello.

He grabbed his own Foxworth-issued phone off the coffee table where he'd left it after the call that had so shaken Cassie. And he thought that if he walked out that door and Cory was standing on the porch, friend or no, he'd deck him. Hard.

Cassie reached for him before her eyes were even fully open and found emptiness. That snapped her fully awake, and she sat up. Stared at where he had been.

She knew she had not dreamed it—the pleasant soreness of various parts of her told her every bit of last night had been real. And just thinking of how she'd acquired that tenderness here and that slightly reddened skin there sent a trembling sort of wanting through her all over again.

She hadn't expected it to be so real. So sweetly, preciously real.

But neither had she expected to wake up alone.

She grabbed the robe that lay across the foot of the bed, although she had to tug it out of the tangled bedclothes. The memory of just how that had happened swept her, and she thought she might need to sit down again under the hot, sweet pressure of it.

He wouldn't have just left. Not Jace. Would he? Had he found waking up with her so awkward he'd gone to avoid any uncomfortable conversation? She couldn't, wouldn't believe it. But when she got up, slid on her warm sheepskin slippers and walked around the bed tugging on the robe, she still felt a pang. So much for her imaginings of a slow, languorous morning with him, exploring even further the amazing fire they could kindle together.

Unless…it hadn't been that way for him? Unless the words he'd spoken in such awe in the darkness faded to mere tokens the morning after?

Telling herself she was being ridiculous, she walked out to the living room, thinking he was likely there, or maybe he'd awakened desperate for coffee and…he was nowhere in the house. She could feel the emptiness. And for a moment her spirits took a nosedive unlike anything she'd felt before. She was nearly reeling. Could she have misjudged him that badly, that he would take off after a night like they'd had? Like some guy out for a quick hookup, nothing more?

That made no sense. No matter what they'd done last night, the reason he was here, the reason he'd come at all, still existed. And Jace would never walk out on that. Because he'd promised.

And then she belatedly realized the house was indeed empty. Not just no Jace, but no Cutter, either. In the same moment she noticed the piece of paper on the kitchen counter, in front of the coffeemaker, which would have been her next stop. She was smiling before she even picked it up.

> *Taking Cutter out. I think he waited as long as he could, but we kind of neglected him last night. J Back in a bit.*

It was signed with one of his quick, clever sketches, a guy who resembled him being pulled by a frantic dog on a leash who looked like Cutter, except for the frantic part.

Her world righted itself, and she reached to put on a pot of coffee for when Jace came home.

Cutter was a very polite walker, but once his business had been attended to, he also was a dog with an obvious goal. He wanted nothing more than to get back to Cassie, maybe even slide back into bed with her before she ever knew he was gone, but that apparently wasn't to be. If it hadn't been for Rafe's admonition—"Trust him"—he might have pushed the issue, but the dog was so determined he gave in, for now, at least.

"What is it you're after, buddy?" he asked the dog as the animal stopped and sat when they reached the end of the block. He looked like he was waiting for something. Or someone. Jace looked across the side street at the undeveloped tract of land that was thick with big trees, where as kids they had often played, and the falling-down cabin where he had gone to hide from his father. "Is our guy hiding out in the woods over here, or what?"

In the instant before a voice came from out of the shadows behind him, Jace saw Cutter rise and sensed... something. He whirled, instinctively dropping into a defensive posture.

"Sort of," came the answer to his question to the dog.

Rafe.

Breathing again, Jace straightened.

"Nice reaction," the man said approvingly as he gravely greeted the dog.

"It would have been better if I'd realized you were there," Jace said flatly.

"Few do." The man said it in the offhand tone of someone who knew it was absolutely true and had no need to brag about it. Rafe looked him up and down. "Looks like you didn't get much sleep."

Jace lowered his gaze quickly. It fell on Cutter, who was, Jace realized, again wearing that expression he could only call smug.

"So," Rafe said to the dog, "chalked up another one?"

The dog's tail wagged. And his expression changed.

Until he'd met Cutter, Jace had never realized dogs could actually smile.

Rafe shifted his gaze back to him. "So. You and Cassie." Jace blinked. "I know his track record. Besides, it's written all over you." Jace felt a little heat in his cheeks, couldn't believe he was actually flushing. "Don't feel bad. I've learned to recognize it by now. Keeps happening all around me."

Jace looked at the other man for a moment. "But never to you?"

Something flickered in the man's expression. "Me? I'm a lost cause, and even he—" he gestured at Cutter "—knows it. He doesn't even try." He gave Jace a small smile. "I suppose he pulled the couch trick? And did a bit of herding?"

Jace blinked. Then, because he couldn't help it, smiled. "Yeah. Yeah, I guess he did."

"He's got it down." Then, briskly, Rafe said, "Tell me more about Cory Grant."

Jace drew back slightly at the abrupt switch. "I... Like what?"

"Like before, first answer that comes to you. What'd he want out of life?"

"No responsibility."

"Plan to get there?"

"Easiest way possible."

"What's stopping him?"

"No drive. No stick-to-it-iveness. No skill except being charming."

Rafe's mouth quirked. "That's enough, for some people." When Jace grimaced, Rafe said, "He sounds almost the opposite of you."

"Especially the charming part," Jace said drily.

"Matter of opinion. But he was still your best friend. Why?"

Jace let out a long breath. "Because he knew the way my father was and still came around. Nobody else had the nerve. And if he was around when my father went off on me, he always tried to distract him."

Rafe nodded after a moment. "So in his way, he looked out for you." Jace nodded. "Who else did he look out for?"

"Cassie, most of all." Jace let out a sigh. "He always swore he'd take care of her, and I think he meant it. That's why it's worrying that he hasn't called her back."

"Brett Dunbar has a contact in Vegas who's checking around. No record of him getting arrested there, but that's about all he's got so far."

Jace nodded.

"Now why don't you get back to her? Women have a thing about that first morning after."

Jace turned away before his face was too readable in the increasing light of morning. But within a few steps he was smiling as, dog in tow, he headed home.

Chapter 16

"You should come with me. Gillian would be happy to see you," Cassidy said as she hefted the big vase of some bright purple sprays of lavender interspersed with soaring white and pink calla lilies.

"I doubt that," Jace said, sounding sour but certain.

"Chuck," she said softly.

He started to protest, then stopped, but still said, "I'll stay by the car, where I can watch Cutter if he alerts to anything." She sighed. "I know, it's a drag and you're tired of the whole thing—"

"No." He blinked. She smiled at him. "If it hadn't been for all this, you might never have come home."

And we never would have had these precious days. And nights. Oh, yes, the nights.

The last three days and nights had been the most amazing of her life. She'd been nervous after that first night, but resolving where they went from there had not been an issue for her. It had been for Jace, however. The next night he had, after they'd finished the pizza they'd ordered on a whim, been so restless he had eventually taken to silently pacing the living room, much as she had previously. She stood it for as long as she could, but the later it got, the more anxious she herself had gotten, and she finally had to break the silence.

"That was good. I hadn't tried that new pizza place yet."

"Mmm."

"And isn't Cutter funny? I've never met a dog that would turn down pepperoni for carrots."

From the far end of the room this time, "Mmm."

"I've got a busy day tomorrow with finalizing all the Thanksgiving arrangement orders, so I need to go in early," she finally said.

"Mmm."

Deciding bluntness was the only course, she stood up. "Jace!" He stopped, turned, staring at her. "I'm going to bed. Are you joining me?"

To her surprise, he had flushed. "I… You…want me to?"

He'd been having the old doubts, she realized. That he could, after what they'd found together, made her angry. "Chuck," she had snapped.

He blinked. "I just…didn't want to assume."

"That after the most amazing night of my life I would want a repeat?"

A slow smile had curved his mouth before he said softly, "It was, wasn't it?"

The night after that, he'd swept her up and carried her to bed before she'd even said a word. "Someday," he'd said, "we'll do a Friday night right, not just hiding in the house."

"And what," she had asked him, "makes you think this isn't doing Friday night exactly right?"

He'd laughed, that deep, solid Jace laugh, and she'd known his father wasn't haunting them any longer, not here, not now. And Jace without doubt was a lover she'd never expected to find.

But she still hadn't been able to convince him to make the Saturday deliveries with her, even though three of the four were people he'd known. He'd driven the shop SUV, but he'd hung back by the car, using the excuse of watching the surroundings. A valid excuse, true, but she had the feeling he was glad to have it.

"Why do you do so many of the deliveries?" he asked when she got back in after the last one.

"I like to. It gets me out, and I like to see people's faces, see their happiness when they get flowers."

"Except maybe that one," he said, jerking his thumb toward the final delivery for the day, which was headed for a funeral.

"No, even that one. It shows them someone cares, someone is thinking about them at a time when they really need to know that. They may not have the emotional capacity at that moment to appreciate it, but eventually it could mean the world to them."

His hand had been on the ignition, but now it dropped away as he turned to look at her. For a long moment, he didn't speak, and her brow furrowed. Then, just as she was about to ask what was wrong, he did.

"You're amazing, Cassidy," he said softly.

He so rarely used her full name she wasn't sure how to take it, except that there had been no mistaking the wonder and appreciation in his voice.

"That's odd," she said when she thought she could

get the words out, "because I was just thinking the same thing about you." For a moment he just held her gaze. And she could see the battle going on behind those vivid blue eyes. "And don't you dare doubt me."

He smiled as she used the phrase she'd so often spoken when she'd been a kid, a couple of years younger than he but still certain she was right about something.

"Why would I when you're usually right?" he said, giving her the same words he had back then.

She couldn't help herself, she reached out to cup his cheek with her hand. He hadn't shaved this morning—they'd been too late getting up after a third incredible night together—and she found to her surprise she liked the look and even the feel of it. It was so…male.

"Careful," he warned, "or we'll end up back in your bed by lunchtime."

"Promise?" she whispered and saw him suck in a harsh breath and swallow.

"Maybe inappropriate, after stopping by a funeral."

"Or maybe most appropriate. Celebrating life."

And again he stared at her. "Amazing," he said, "was an understatement."

"Back at you," she said, smiling at him now.

And then Cutter gave a bark from the back seat, so obviously happy they both laughed.

They made it before lunchtime.

"I could get used to Sunday mornings like this," Jace said, yawning and stretching widely as he rubbed a hand absently over his bare chest.

"So could I." Cassie's tone was far too intent for

the toast she was spreading butter on, and he looked over to find her watching him. Her gaze slid from his chest downward, until he was very aware that with one tug she could have these old sweats off him. And she looked as if, despite the night they'd again spent exploring every aspect of the fire they kindled together, that was exactly what she wanted to do.

He felt the muscles of his abdomen tighten in response, while parts farther down quickly awoke to possibilities.

"Eat first," she said, not bothering to deny what they both knew was coming. "Besides," she added with a teasing smile, "you need to keep up your strength."

He grinned back, feeling better than he ever had in his life. "And you. I'll do my best to wear you out."

"I think you might just be able to," she said, her voice matching that smile as she went back to buttering the last slice of toast. "In fifty or sixty years or so."

He went very still. Fifty or sixty years. A lifetime from now. Spent with Cassie, holding her, loving her. He felt suddenly as he had when his father used to dangle some much-wanted temptation in front of him, only to pull it back with a harsh laugh and declare him unworthy of it. And gradually Jace had learned it was best not to let the man know he wanted anything.

It had not been much of a transition from that to not allowing himself to want anything in the first place.

But he had somehow slipped up this time. He wanted Cassie. This was too powerful, too strong to deny, no matter how he tried to tamp it down, no matter that he'd spent the week he'd been here trying not to think about it.

And now, with a single, short sentence, she seemed to be offering it to him.

Whoa, there, Cahill. Don't be a bigger fool than you already are.

"You'd be tired of me in a month," he said flatly.

Her head came up sharply. She stared at him. "Are you saying I have a short attention span?"

He drew back slightly. "I... No. Of course not. I just... What you said sounded like..."

"Forever?" Her voice had softened.

"Yes. And I know you don't want that."

She studied him for a moment. "With you, you mean."

He let out a compressed breath. He didn't want to fight with her. Especially didn't want her fighting with him. How had they gone from such warm, peaceful intimacy to this?

Because you forgot who you are. And aren't.

"Chuck." Cassie snapped it out harshly.

He blinked. Then shook his head slowly. "It's not him, it's the truth. I've got nothing and I can offer you nothing, Cassie."

"And you are nothing? Is that it?"

"Close enough," he said, the old bitterness he'd thought behind him biting deep.

"How can you still let him own you like that?"

"Maybe he was right all along."

"Be careful what you say, Cahill. This may only be a butter knife, but it could do some damage."

He swallowed. She looked fierce enough to use the thing on him, all right. And her voice had taken on that sarcastic tone he remembered from all those years ago, usually from when she was about to take someone apart with some devastatingly logical and accurate argument.

"Why do you think my brother chose you to make that promise?" she asked.

He frowned at the seeming non sequitur, since it seemed obvious to him. "I was his friend."

"He had friends still here in town. It would have been a lot easier to pick one of them, who would already be here, wouldn't it? But no, he picked you, who ended up a thousand miles away."

He felt a little silly that that had never even occurred to him.

"And why?" she snapped out. "Because even my stupid brother knew you were the one who would keep that promise."

"Anybody would—"

"Like anybody would spend ten years of their life working off debts that weren't even theirs? Don't even try to sell that one."

He'd forgotten how fierce she could be. And it belatedly occurred to him that she wasn't fighting him, not really. She was fighting for him. And that was novelty enough that he couldn't think of a thing to say.

"I've heard people tell women," she went on, her voice gentler now, "that if you want to know how a man will treat you, watch how he treats his mother. I'd say you get top of the class in that."

"Cassie," he began, then stopped because he still couldn't think of a thing to say.

"Now, if you're past that bit of idiocy, letting that… creature have the slightest say in who you are, let's have breakfast."

Idiocy. Yeah, that fit, all right. Sometimes he was one.

Especially around her.

They ate in silence. The mood seemed suddenly as gray as the November day outside. When he finished, Cassidy watched as he carried his plate, silverware and coffee mug to the sink, rinsed them and put them in the dishwasher. Then he came back for hers, except for the mug, since she hadn't finished her coffee yet. While she did he went for the skillet she'd fixed eggs in, the bowl and whisk she'd used, and did the same with them. This was clearly something he did without thought; it needed to be done, so he did it.

Then he picked up the butter knife. Looked at it for a long moment. There was a solid thump as she put her mug down on the counter.

"I won't apologize," she said, rather fiercely.

"I didn't expect you to."

"Sometimes I wish he was here so I could use that on him," she said, gesturing at the knife.

"I don't," he said, appearing to suppress a shudder. "I wouldn't want him anywhere around you."

"I wish you had the same protective instinct about yourself. Then maybe you'd quit carrying him around in your head."

He put both hands on the edge of the sink and stared out the window. "I try. But sometimes he sneaks back in."

"Of course he does. Even if he was never your dad, he was your father."

She knew he'd understand what she meant, because long ago, during a period when she'd been chafing a bit at her father's restrictions, he'd told her she was lucky to have a father and a dad both in one.

"My mother's taken to calling him the sperm donor."

Cassidy laughed. "Has she? Good for her."

"She always liked you."

"And I her." She meant it, even if she had wished now and then that the woman would stand up for her son more.

"She used to say she hoped you met a good man, one worthy of you."

Did she know it would be you?

Cassidy bit back the words even though she wanted to say them. But the memory of the sudden, frozen stillness of him after she'd joked about fifty or sixty years stilled her tongue. For once.

"And I used to think that whoever he was, he'd be a lucky guy," Jace said softly, still not looking at her. "He'd have a great life. And never be bored."

He'd thought of her like that, even then? She felt a tightness in her chest, all the words she wanted to say piling up in her throat. She tried to pick the safest, something that wouldn't shatter this unexpected sweetness.

A break in the clouds outside sent a sudden ray of sunlight in through the kitchen window, lighting him up like a spotlight. She stared at him, standing there, seeing both the clean precision of his profile and the tension in his jaw. His fingers were tight on the edge of the sink, knuckles white.

She could not even begin to imagine what he carried with him from that childhood, couldn't begin to understand what it was like. Not when she'd been so lucky herself to have had her wonderful parents for so long.

She saw him draw in a deep breath. And then, as if it were a conscious effort, as she thought it likely was, he relaxed.

"It's clearing out," he said, still looking out the window.

"Maybe we'll have one of those freakishly clear, sunny Thanksgiving days," she said, carrying her now-empty mug over to the dishwasher. "Like that year you came and spent it with us."

He looked at her then, a smile lifting one corner of his mouth. So he did still have some good memories of those days. "That was the best Thanksgiving ever," he said. It had been so nice they'd actually been outside most of the day, soaking up the rare November sunshine.

She remembered vividly when Jace had begun, without request or suggestion, to carry things out to the table. Cory had gotten on his case about being so dutiful. Jace had turned on him and said, "If you don't appreciate this, what you've got, you're an idiot."

She knew she hadn't been meant to hear it, but she'd been in the doorway, about to come in. She'd fallen even more in love with him that day. And she'd spent the rest of the day in a fifteen-year-old girly haze, fantasizing that one day he'd look at her and fall as crazy in love with her.

And less than two years later, he'd been gone.

She looked away quickly, afraid of what might be showing in her face. She gave closing up the dishwasher much more attention than it required. When she finally risked a glance at him, he was still staring out the window, but his expression had changed. He was frowning, in that Jace way that told her he was working on something in that head of his.

And when he finally turned to look at her, she knew the wheels were turning quickly. "There was something else in your jacket pocket besides that, wasn't there?" he asked, gesturing at the lever that sat on the kitchen counter, as if having it there in sight would help them figure out what Cory had been trying to say.

She frowned. "Just a broken piece of an evergreen branch."

"What did you do with it?"

"I tossed it in the trash box of burnable stuff we started in there."

Jace turned abruptly and headed for the hall. More than curious now, she followed. He found the box—which she figured would be filled and refilled time and again before she got done—reached into it and came up with the small piece of greenery.

"Redwood," he murmured, in a tone of discovery that seemed odd given there were many of the trees around here.

"Jace?" she asked.

He turned to her then. "That Thanksgiving, remember Cory and I took off for the woods, to find some branches for your mom to make a wreath after she talked about wanting to do it?"

"Of course I do. It thrilled her. Especially since you let Cory take the credit when I know darn well it was your idea." He looked a little taken aback. She rolled her eyes. "Please. As if he would ever."

"Oh."

He gave her a sheepish smile. At that moment she thought it the sweetest expression she'd ever seen. Which would embarrass the heck out of him, so she merely said, "What about it?"

Instantly he was back to that intent expression. "That day, we went all the way to the old cabin."

He meant, she knew, the remains of an old cabin that had been abandoned decades ago, long before the large tract of forest had become public land. When the crumbling structure had proved too great a temptation for local kids, and the county had said it was months, maybe years away on their to-do list, some parents—led by her father—had gotten together and torn it down far enough that the hazard was greatly lessened.

"And?" she prompted.

"There are a few redwoods near there. Especially around the old well house."

She looked at the small piece of branch. This time she said nothing, and after a moment he continued.

"Cory went poking around that well house. The old holding tank was still there, but all rusted out on the back side against the wall."

He reached out and picked up the lever from the counter. Looked at it for a moment, then at her. She just waited silently. And finally he drew a deep breath and went on.

"He said that would be a great place to hide something, if you ever needed to."

Cassidy drew back slightly. "You think…" she began.

"I'm not sure what I think," he said. "I'm just saying… possibilities." He shook his head. "It's…crazy. And probably not…"

"Spell it out for me," she said, suspecting he'd made one of those leaps. "Lay the pieces out in order."

He drew in another deep breath. "Cory's here four months ago but spends most of his time not here. Four months ago that gang gets ripped off. Cory takes off again. Gang leader and his brother are in jail, but the brother gets out. Right after that, you pick up a stalker. Who appears not to be after you yourself, but mostly watching. Then he risks breaking in to search Cory's room. And then you find this—" he held up the lever "—in the pocket of a jacket you'd surely miss and go looking for, in that same room."

She followed his thought process. She saw how he'd gotten there, like a long row of dominoes toppling, but it was so incredible she couldn't quite believe it.

"But why would he ever think I would know what that lever meant?"

"He wouldn't. But he probably figured I would."

She stared at him. Wondered if he fully understood yet what he'd just admitted, that even her scapegrace brother had known he was solid to the core, that Cory had known with utter certainty that if she got into trouble, Jace would be here to make this connection.

That her brother had left her with that trouble was something she'd have to take up with him.

If he ever dared to come back, that is.

Chapter 17

"I'm going to hunt my brother down and skewer him," Cassie said fiercely.

"I'll help," Jace said, still staring at the lever. "He had no business pulling you into the middle of…whatever the hell this is."

And it made him angrier than he'd been in a while to think of what Cory had done so heedlessly. Apparently.

"If I'm right, of course," he amended quickly. "I could be way wrong. You know I go off on…tangents sometimes."

"Sometimes tangents hold the answer." She said it simply, as if it were obvious to everyone. "Only one way to find out," she said briskly.

"Yeah. I'll go take a look."

"You'll go? I think you mean we'll go."

Jace shook his head. "You should stay here, with Cutter."

"While you trek out there alone? I don't think so."

"It's only at the end of the street."

"And he was inside this house four days ago."

"And we haven't seen a sign of him since," Jace countered.

"Then it's safe for both of us to go."

He opened his mouth, then shut it again. Leave it to Cassie to take his efforts at persuasion and turn them back on him.

"I don't want you getting hurt," he finally said.

"Did you ever stop to think that maybe I don't want *you* getting hurt, on my account?"

He blinked. Actually, he hadn't, not in exactly that way. And now that she'd said it, he couldn't deny how that bit of possessive protectiveness felt. Good. Darn good.

"Let's go. I'll bet proof you're right is sitting in an old well tank right down there," she said, gesturing north.

Her faith nearly shattered him. Something must have shown in his face, because she was suddenly in his arms, hugging him. And he was hugging her back, fighting down the feeling that if he had this, if he had her to hold him like this, he could keep going forever, no matter what. That he could take the numbness of having to dull his mind at whatever job he was working, as long as he had her acceptance to come back to. It was a feeling much bigger than what they'd discovered in her bed, and that realization shook him more than a little.

His head came up, and he met her smiling face and those gold-flecked eyes. He let out a long, low breath. Something changed in her gaze then, shifted to the kind of warmth and welcome he'd never expected to see in them, the kind he'd seen there when she'd spoken those words that had shattered him down to his soul.

I have wanted you since the first day I saw you...

"Do you suppose we have time?" she asked, and there was no mistaking what she was suggesting.

"I do," he said rather wryly, "but you'd probably end up a bit shortchanged."

"I doubt that." She was practically purring, and it was all Jace could do not to take her up on it right here and now.

"Damn, Cassie. You fry every circuit."

Her smile was brilliant. And it seemed to light him up inside as much as it lit up her lovely face.

"Well, let's go. Proving you right is only a couple of blocks away!" she exclaimed.

She sounded so utterly confident it warmed him all over again, but in the back of his mind that voice still lingered, telling him this was just one of those leaps his brain made. That he thought strangely, wrongly, stupidly, and had no mental discipline.

Cassie came around the kitchen counter and leaned against him. "Chuck," she whispered.

His gaze shot to her face. Her expression was full of both support and warning. If it hadn't been so uncanny, how she always seemed to know when he slipped back into those paths, he would have laughed.

"You've figured it out, I know it."

"I hope you're right."

"I am. Just like I know you'd never let anything happen to me."

"Yes," he said, meaning it. She might want to catch this guy, but his priority was to keep her safe. More now than ever. Before it had been because of a promise made to a friend. Now it was much, much bigger. More crucial. More essential.

And then his mind fired one of those crazy thoughts at him—that not only did her life depend on him keeping her safe, so did his.

Cassie hadn't simply taken a walk for a long while. She used to enjoy it but hadn't had time for such relaxing pursuits for a long time. Since the day her parents had been killed, in fact, now that she thought about it.

She wasn't actually enjoying it now, because the moment they'd left the house, Cutter had morphed from the comforting companion to something else entirely. Something a lot less sweet and a lot more intimidating. He was clearly on guard. But she also realized that with Jace and Cutter by her side, she didn't feel in the least threatened.

Jace, on the other hand, was so silent she knew something was bothering him. She suspected it was as much that they might find nothing as anything else. His father deserved to be…something. Right now she couldn't think of anything fitting enough.

She waited as a car passed them on the street, then mused aloud, "I wonder how Edison's father felt."

Jace seemed to snap out of his thoughts to look at her. "What?"

"Just wondering how Thomas Edison's father felt when the kid they said was too stupid to learn anything ended up getting credit for inventing just about everything."

"He stole most of it from Tesla," Jace said.

"I know." She looked up at him then, grinning, because he'd said exactly what she'd expected him to say. "But he was very clever about it."

"And ruthless." To her delight, he was laughing as he said it.

Cutter, who had been alertly sniffing the air as they reached the edge of the trees, his ears swiveling as he listened, too, paused in his work for a moment to look up at them. He was on Jace's side and shifted suddenly to brush up against him. But it must have been more than a mere brush, because Jace had to take a sideways step to keep his balance. Which brought him up against her side. As if that had been his goal, the dog went back to his task.

Jace laughed again, said, "Yeah, yeah," to the dog. But he put his arm around her shoulders, and Cassie made a mental note to give the dog his beloved carrots when they got back.

She slipped her arm around his lean waist and wished she could freeze this moment in time. Walking through the quiet forest of tall trees, Jace not just beside her but with her, in all the ways she'd ever wished for. She knew the moments ahead, when they reached the old cabin, could change everything. And as much as she wanted to know the truth about Cory, she wanted to keep this feeling more. Much, much more.

She tried to reason it out as they went. They would either find something in the well house or not. If not, things would go on as they were, for a while, at least. A very tempting prospect. One that put her a bit at war with her desire to clear this up—if this went on, Jace would stay. And right now she wasn't certain she didn't want that more than anything else.

If they did find something, what happened would depend on what it was. If it was indeed proof Cory had done something beyond foolish—something she now had to admit her brother was entirely capable of—then there would be the deciding what to do about it. She felt a little chill; Detective Dunbar had said Foxworth cooperated with the police, so did that mean that if it were, for example, the stolen money, they would tell the police Cory had likely taken it?

She forced down the unwelcome thoughts. Her mother had always cautioned her about opening the door for trouble before it had even knocked, and it was a bit of wisdom she tried to live by; no sense in wasting energy worrying about things that hadn't happened. Her father had a slightly different view, more of a proviso, he'd always said.

Prepare for the worst and then hope for the best.
And enjoy the present.

The image of her parents' exchange flashed into her mind with vivid clarity. Sometimes she still missed them so much it was a dull, hollow ache inside. And the only thing she'd ever found to really ease it at all was... Jace. Jace, who would probably leave as soon as this was resolved.

And suddenly she wanted to turn around, run the other way.

"Cassie?"

She realized belatedly that she had stopped walking. And that Jace was looking at her quizzically.

"I'm just…worried about what we'll find."

"Me, too."

She gave a half-hearted laugh. "You're worried we'll find nothing. I'm worried we'll find…something."

"But don't you want this over with?"

Not if it means you'll go. "I don't want my brother in as much trouble as this might be."

"Then we'll deal."

We. He'd said it so easily she had to rein in her hopes that he meant that in a more solid sense than he likely did. Whatever happened, whatever they found and whatever was to be done with it, Jace would stick to the end.

But at the end, he would go. Hadn't he made that clear? He thought he had nothing to offer. While she thought what he had to offer was more than enough, it was going to take more than a few days to convince him of that. Which she wasn't going to get.

"I'm tired of dealing," she said wearily, in that moment meaning it more than she ever had. "Sometimes I want to just dump it all and run away."

"I hear that," Jace said softly.

She sighed. "You have a lot more reason than I do."

"No. I don't."

"But—"

"Do you really think having a father like mine is worse than having parents like yours and then losing them?"

"Yes. Because at least I had them for twenty-two years. All you had was a fool who couldn't—or wouldn't—see the treasure he had in his own son."

His arm tightened around her for a moment, as if

he couldn't think of anything to say but wanted her to know he'd heard—and appreciated?—her words.

"You know what I'd really like?" He stopped in his tracks to look down at her. Something flashed in the blue depths of his eyes, and she couldn't help smiling. "Besides that," she agreed.

The smile she got back made her hopes soar again and gave her the courage to finish saying what she'd begun.

"I wish we could leave it all behind. Start fresh."

He stopped in his tracks at the end of the narrow path through the trees; they were at the edge of the clearing where the old cabin had stood. But instead of shutting down at the idea of *we*, he only said, "You'd leave the shop?"

"I love it, but because it was theirs. Sometimes it feels like a weight I can't shed."

"They…wouldn't want that."

She stared at him. For all her wrestling with the frequent urge to jettison it all, she'd never fully formed that thought in her head. She'd always assumed they would want her to keep it going. Had assumed they'd wanted it to stay in the family and had turned down offers to buy her out more than once.

"They wanted you happy more than anything," Jace added, as if he thought she didn't believe him.

"You're right," she whispered. "They did."

"And you're trying to do alone what it took the two of them to do." His mouth tightened. "Thanks to Cory."

Abruptly she snapped back to the present, and why they were here. And suddenly she did want this over with. She wanted to know where she stood, with her brother and more importantly with Jace.

"Let's go."

It came out a little abruptly, and Jace drew back slightly. "I didn't mean—"

"I know." She took a deep breath to steady herself. "I've been stalling, Jace. I didn't want this to end, because I didn't want you to leave. More than ever…now." She knew, by that flash in his eyes again, he realized she meant after the incredible three nights they'd had together. "But until this is over, everything is in limbo. And I don't like that."

"You never did," he said quietly.

No, she hadn't. So she started walking again, glancing toward the flattened cabin but heading for the small, square shedlike structure that was the well house. Jace said nothing more, although she could almost hear his mind racing.

When she got there, she pulled the door open. Cutter made a low noise, not quite a growl. She wondered if he scented the creature of the rodent persuasion who had obviously been living in here, at one time, anyway. The old holding tank was there, listing to one side.

She leaned in, saw what Jace had described, the rusted out hole in the back. She started to reach, but a hand on her shoulder stayed her.

"Let me." She looked up at him. "It's rusty. If you got cut, it could get nasty."

"So we'll let you get cut instead?" she asked, her tone slightly scoffing.

"Yes." He said it firmly. "Besides, my arms are longer."

She couldn't argue that and eased back as he shouldered past her. Carefully, almost gently, but determined.

"Anything?" she asked after a moment of him feeling around.

"I don't want to think about what my hand's in," he muttered, "but there's something…hang on…ah."

He pulled his arm back. In his hand was a bundle wrapped in a piece of plastic tarp. It was about six inches high and wide and about ten inches long, and water from the tank dripped from it. And his shirtsleeve was soaked nearly to the elbow.

For a long moment she just stared. The part of her that was delighted Jace had been right despite his doubts warred with the fear building inside her that her brother had done something very, very stupid.

Backing out of the confines of the well house, Jace put the package on the ground. The tarp was sealed shut with several wide strips of tape. And she had a sudden flash of memory.

"Cory asked me for packing tape," she said, her voice barely above a whisper. "I told him all I had was at the shop. He came to get it. It was the only time he set foot there."

She heard her own words come out choppily, heard how stunned she sounded. Jace's arm came around her again. The dry one, she noticed vaguely. Even now, he thought of that.

"It's about the right size," Jace said, studying the wrapped package.

The money stolen from that Seattle gang. Was that what was in there, cash? He was right—the dimensions would fit several stacks of bills. And everything she'd been thinking about, worried about, flooded back. What would happen now, what would they do, what would Rafe—and Detective Dunbar—do?

"Cassie—"

Jace was cut off by a fierce, rumbling growl from Cutter. The dog's ears and nose were both pointed to their left. Then the dog whirled and jumped back to stand between them and whatever he'd scented or heard.

On guard.

The dog obviously hadn't forgotten his job. And she knew instinctively that Cutter would die carrying it out, if he had to. And then she looked at Jace, and what she saw in his face told her the same thing about him. She shivered. She could not even bear the thought. Because Jace dead would destroy her world all over again.

Cutter looked as if he would give anything to be able to go after whatever—or whoever—was coming toward them. His growl escalated to a cascade of snarling that would scare off any sane person.

Except, perhaps, the one that stepped out of the woods barely six feet away. The man she'd seen so often. The man who so resembled his brother in prison. The man in the photo.

The man with a pistol in his hand.

Chapter 18

It all happened so fast Jace had no time to think. He just reacted. The man raised the gun. He pushed Cassie behind the well house. Cutter gave him an odd, split-second look, then broke left at a run, letting out an ear-splitting string of snarls and barks. Jace's brain instantly registered he'd seen that pattern from the animal before. That night in the alley, at the shop. And just as then, the man's attention went with the snarling, vicious-looking animal. With it went the weapon, tracking the dog.

Cutter's giving you a chance.

Jace launched himself at the man. A shot nearly deafened him as he hit him low and hard. All he could do was pray it hadn't hit Cutter. Or Cassie, somehow. He felt something hard strike a glancing blow on his forehead. Realized the guy had swung back with the weapon as they went down to the forest floor. He guessed, grabbed, caught the barrel of the gun and wrenched at it hard. At the same time he slammed his other elbow into the man's throat, had the satisfaction of hearing him gurgle, then gasp for air. More importantly, he lost his grip on the weapon and Jace tossed it out of reach.

But the action of removing the weapon made him vulnerable for an instant, and the man took advantage. He hit Jace's jaw hard, snapping his head back. And Jace suddenly realized he was wrestling with the guy. And he'd never been a wrestler.

He let go. Rolled off the man. Went to his knees, then stood in one smooth motion. In the same moment, the other man did the same, but much less smoothly. He saw the shift in balance in the instant before the man charged.

Let it flow.

Mr. Bradley's words echoed in his mind. He took the split second he had to change his mind-set, and almost without conscious thought his body readied.

And when the man charged, Jace grabbed, gripped and threw him neatly over his shoulder. He landed flat on his back with a grunt, and Jace could tell by his face and gasping effort at breathing that he'd had the wind knocked out of him.

Then Cutter was there. The sight of a set of intimidating fangs and the sound of the dog's ferocious, warning growl tipped the scales. The man gave up with a groan. And then Jace saw that there had been another factor; Cassie was just a few feet away, with the man's own weapon in her hands, aimed at the top of the man's shaved head. Relieved to see that the shot he'd heard had gone wild, not hitting anyone, Jace rubbed at his jaw.

"Are you all right?" Cassie asked, and the deep, genuine concern took the chill out of the November air.

"Fine." Relatively speaking. It could have been worse. A lot worse.

"Now what?" Cassie asked, edging toward him.

Jace looked at the man on the ground. "You could just shoot him. Nobody'd blame you."

As the man gasped for air to breathe, he held up his hands, palms out, shaking his head. At the same time, Cassie gave him a startled look, as if she couldn't believe he'd really said that. He winked at her. She got it immediately and looked back at the man.

"I suppose I could."

The man's eyes widened in terror now. "No," he managed to gasp out. "No, don't."

"They won't. But I might," came a voice from the trees. They all looked as Rafe stepped into the clearing from exactly the spot Schiff had come from.

"You were there all along," Cassie exclaimed.

"I was a ways back, but I was around."

Jace was beginning to think that for Rafe, "around" meant many different things. And then he noticed that slung over Rafe's right shoulder was a very lethal-looking rifle, with a very professional-looking scope. This, Jace thought, was no mere hunting rifle. He glanced at the man on the ground, then back at Rafe, who was studying the man intently. And that man had taken one look at Rafe and fallen silent again. So maybe that's exactly what the rifle was. It was just that Rafe was no ordinary hunter.

On that thought Rafe looked at Jace. "I figured you and Cutter could handle it, but a little insurance never hurts."

That vote of confidence, from this man, meant more to Jace than he could put into words at the moment. So he only nodded, but Rafe seemed to understand.

"That was smooth. You ever want a sparring partner, we've got a guy," he said conversationally as he reached into an outside pocket of the pack he'd dropped off his left shoulder and pulled out some heavy-duty zip ties. He efficiently bound the man's ankles, rolled him onto his stomach and fastened his wrists behind him.

"Ow," the man protested.

"Shut up or I'll use the third one to fasten those two together," Rafe said mildly. The idea of being hog-tied apparently did not appeal, because the man shut up.

Jace rubbed at his jaw and muttered, "Maybe you'll get a cell close to your brother, so you can chat."

The man's eyes widened, and Jace realized he hadn't expected them to know who he was.

Then Rafe turned to Cassie, who was holding Schiff's pistol as if it were sizzling.

"Want me to take that?" he asked in a gentle tone Jace had never heard from him.

"Yes, please," she said gratefully. "I'm glad I didn't have to use it, since I don't have a clue about handguns."

"This one's basically point and shoot," Rafe said as he took it and did something that made the rack of bullets slide out of the grip. Then he worked the slide and ejected one more, caught it and shoved it all into a plastic baggie he pulled out of a pocket above where the zip ties had come from. Foxworth, it seemed, was prepared for anything.

"Be interesting to see if ballistics on that turn up anywhere," Rafe said. "Bet it's in some police record, somewhere, for something."

Cassie had been looking at Schiff. And she laughed,

although it sounded a bit strained. "Judging by the look that just went across his face, I'd say you're right."

"Cutter, guard," Rafe said. The dog gave him a look that Jace could only describe as sour.

Cassie laughed again, but it was better this time. "Was that the canine equivalent of 'duh'?" she asked.

Rafe grinned at her. It was a brief, flashing expression, but in that moment he looked like a different man. "Pretty much," he agreed.

"You know," Jace said slowly, thinking this was going to sound crazy, "there was an instant there when he looked up at me, right before he did exactly what he did that night behind the flower shop... It almost felt like he was trying to tell me he was going to do it again."

"He was," Rafe said easily. "And better yet, he trusted you to get it."

Jace felt nearly as warmed as he'd felt when Rafe had said he trusted him.

"What happens now?" Cassie said. Her voice sounded off again, and he looked at her, trying to figure out why. "Do we open that?" She gestured at the package that lay on the ground. "Or do you have to...turn it over to someone?"

"I think we can at least see what it is."

Rafe pulled a folding knife out of a sheath on his belt and snapped it open. Then, to Jace's surprise, he held it out to him. "You're the one who tossed that clown like a sack of beans. You want to do the honors?"

He took the blade and knelt beside the package. He slit the tape carefully and unfolded the plastic tarp.

There was more plastic wrapped several times around what the package held, but it was clear and the contents were easily visible.

Jace let out a low whistle. He'd never seen this much cash at one time in person before. But then something in one corner of the big bundle caught his eye, a square of white. A folded piece of paper. And it had Cassie's name on it. In Cory's handwriting.

She'd apparently seen it at the same moment, because he heard her breath catch. Instinctively he reached to slice the package open and retrieve the paper. But he paused to glance at Rafe.

"Just cut out the note, don't open the whole thing," he said. "Until we decide what to do."

Jace nodded and made two neat cuts. He slid out the folded sheet of what he now saw was the reverse side of a printed form. He stood up and held it out to Cassie. She shook her head, somewhat fiercely. It hit him suddenly, belatedly, that she had just been confronted with proof positive that her brother had gotten involved in something way over his head. No wonder she had sounded out of it.

He crossed the two feet between them in a stride and pulled her into his arms. "I'm sorry," he whispered.

"But not surprised," she said with a sigh.

"No. Not really."

"Read it," she said.

"You're sure you don't want to—"

"Yes. Very."

He let go of her with his right arm but continued to

hold her with his left. He flipped the folded page open with his thumb.

It was a year-end balance sheet. From the florist shop, dated almost a year ago. And the numbers were not good. But he barely noticed, distracted by the scrawl in the clear space in the lower left corner.

> *That place is sucking the life out of you, Cass.*
> *I'm sorry I can't stay to help, but this should take*
> *care of you for a long time if you're careful. Get*
> *out of there. I love you.*
> *Cory*

He let out a long breath. And then looked at her.

"It was him, wasn't it?"

He only nodded. He had no words, in fact no concept of what she was feeling now, and he knew it. But he also knew she was hurting, badly, and he hugged her, held her, letting out a silent curse in his mind at the man who had once been his best friend.

Cassidy made a low, choking sound. "I don't know whether to laugh or cry. This is so…twisted."

She'd finally asked to see her brother's note, and Jace had held it out for her to read.

"If this is Cory's version of taking care of you, yeah, it is," Jace muttered.

"Where did he get the idea that I would ever take this money?" she asked with the first spark of anger. She welcomed it.

"Same place he got the idea to steal it, I'd guess."

"Down in the depths of stupidity?" Cassidy suggested, feeling stronger now.

"He swam there now and then," Jace said wryly.

She looked at Rafe, who had been examining the money. Now that she knew it was stacks of hundreds, the bundle seemed somehow even bigger.

"I'd say quarter of a million," Rafe said.

The number stunned her. "What on earth do we do with it? Give it back?"

Rafe looked at her. "To a gang of criminals?"

She'd almost forgotten that part. She sighed. Then she looked at Jace. "You should take it," she said impulsively. "Pay off whatever's left of the debt your father left."

"Are you serious?" he nearly yelped. "That's something my father would do."

Cassidy sighed. "I'm sorry. I knew that you would never do that the moment I said it." He would never, ever go down the path Cory had chosen, no matter the temptation, no matter the hardship. Jace was exactly who she'd always known he was.

More calmly, he said, "My mother would kick my ass from here to Alaska if I ever took dirty money for her. Besides, it is paid off. That was her phone call—she got the last statement, zeroed out."

She stared at him with no small amount of awe. But she'd have to wait to tell him that—right now they had other things to deal with.

"What about the people it was stolen from?" she asked Rafe. "Is there a way to find them, to give it back?"

"From what Brett said, most of their cash came from dealing drugs," Rafe answered. "Not sure that qualifies as stolen."

"Leave it to Cory," Jace said, shaking his head.

"Foxworth works for you," Rafe said to Cassidy. "And it's likely there's not a specific victim to return this to. Maybe a few could be isolated, though. Brett said there were rumors of a protection racket."

"Then it should go to them," Cassidy said quickly, and Jace nodded in agreement.

Rafe held up a hand. "But it's also evidence."

Cassidy felt a chill. "Against my brother."

"I'm not sure where stealing what's already stolen or extorted falls, even if you did know where your brother is. But it could be evidence against who he stole it from."

"The gang?" Cassidy perked up at that; putting more people like that in jail seemed like a good idea.

"Let me make a call," Rafe said. "We've got a guy who can advise us. Legally, I mean." He took out the phone like theirs and hit two numbers. A moment later he said, "Katie? Rafe." A pause. "Fine. And thanks, but Cutter and I will be good. Is Gavin there?" This time the pause was a bare second. "Sorry, did I interrupt?"

Cassidy immediately thought of another time when Rafe had asked that question, when she and Jace had been...busy. Heat flooded her, but it was followed by a slight chill as she realized that, except for these details, this was essentially over and now she was going to have to face what would happen—or not happen—next with herself and Jace.

She tried to focus on Rafe's succinct account of what had happened. Then Rafe listened for a long moment before saying, "Yeah, Brett's got some contacts. And he's read in." Another pause. "Okay." He moved as if he were going to end the call, but then added, "Sorry about the interruption, de Marco. As you were."

He was smiling when he did end the call. A kind of wistful smile Cassidy had seen on his face once before. But then her brain put together two things he'd said and it blasted all other thought out of her head.

"De Marco? Gavin? *The* Gavin de Marco?" she exclaimed.

Jace drew back, whistled. "'We've got a guy'?"

"Yeah." Rafe looked at Jace and said cryptically, "He was number nine." His gaze flicked to Cutter, back to Jace, then her, then back to Jace again. Jace obviously understood what he meant, because his eyes widened.

"So now what?" Cassidy asked, figuring she'd find out what the mysterious exchange had been about later. "We call Detective Dunbar?"

Rafe nodded. "And dump it all in his lap." A wry smile crossed his face. "It won't be the first time. He always manages to work through it."

Working through it, Cassidy found by the time darkness fell, was a long, complicated process involving photographs of the scene, the well house, the tank and the money in place. Once they had finished at the scene, they had gone to Foxworth headquarters, where she welcomed both the comfort of the homey room downstairs and the warmth of the fireplace there. Clearly at home here, Cutter hopped up on one end of the couch. Since

Rafe and Dunbar had been in the flanking chairs, that left only the spot next to her for Jace.

Just like he did with you.

But the thought didn't linger as they continued the process, including her and Jace giving detailed statements, where the main thing she found to be happy about was being able to say honestly she had no idea where Cory was.

Detective Dunbar had been businesslike but kind, and he seemed to understand her tension when the subject had turned to her brother.

"Cory's got faults, a lot of them, but I never realized he was so off center he'd think this was a good idea," she'd said sadly.

"He didn't think at all," Jace had said rather sharply, "or he would have realized what he could be bringing down on you with this insane scheme."

And then, Cassidy remembered as she soaked up the warmth of the fire even though it was making her sleepy, had come another annoying round of pointed male glances; Dunbar had looked from Jace to her, then to Cutter on the floor near him, and finally to Rafe, who had nodded as if in confirmation. And then the sheriff's detective had smiled and reached out to scratch behind Cutter's right ear familiarly.

Then the detective had disappeared to make some calls to his contacts, and Rafe had disappeared into the kitchen, probably to make more of the coffee he seemed to run on, even at this hour. No wonder he didn't sleep much, Cassidy thought now, smothering a yawn.

But then he reappeared and handed her a mug that, to her surprise, was filled with hot chocolate.

"It took Hayley—my boss's wife—to convince me not everybody drinks coffee at 10:00 p.m."

"Thank you," she said, taking the mug. "Is it? Really? Ten, I mean?"

"Little after," Rafe said, sipping at his own mug, which she was sure held coffee.

For a while they sat in the Foxworth gathering room in silence, watching the fire, each seemingly sorting out their own thoughts.

"I can't believe it's over," Cassidy said eventually. "In…a week."

"Foxworth is obviously efficient," Jace said, lifting his mug to Rafe.

"You held your own," Rafe said, and Cassidy could have hugged him for the appreciation in Jace's eyes. And she wondered if perhaps Rafe had let Jace handle it, as if he somehow sensed Jace needed to know he could. Rafe shifted his gaze to her. "They know the money's gone now, and it's cost Schiff—he'll be on his way back to jail. They should likely back off, but you should still be aware."

Cassidy paled. "You think they might still…"

"It would be stupid," Rafe said. "But then…" He gave a shrug that said everything about his assessment of the Schiff brothers' stupidity. Then he looked back at Jace. "What will you do now?"

Caught off guard by the unexpected plunge into territory she'd been tiptoeing around, Cassidy's hands tightened around the warm mug even though she was no longer cold.

But you might be again. Soon.

"I don't know," Jace said. "My mom's doing okay now."

"You have a job to get back to?" Rafe asked.

Jace's mouth quirked. "Maybe. One, anyway. Other two weren't big on unscheduled time off."

Cassidy's breath caught. It had been bad enough that he'd been working three jobs, but he'd quit two of them to come help her?

"Pretty rigid, huh?" Rafe asked.

Jace nodded, then said wryly, "Not something I do well with."

"That thinking outside the box?"

Jace nodded, and Cassidy realized that these two must have had quite a talk at some point. A few moments later, Rafe excused himself to make yet another call.

Cassidy waited until she no longer could. And then she hated the almost pleading note that came into her voice. "Can you…at least stay through Thanksgiving? Maybe your mom could come up? Mrs. Alston is coming—she always liked your mom—and May from the shop and her little boy. We'll have a nice dinner. I'd like an excuse to make Mom's potatoes, and a nice turkey and a nice—"

She stopped herself at the third *nice*. Lowered her gaze to her hands as she let out a long breath.

"Mom would love to see you," Jace said quietly. "But a plane ticket right now isn't in the cards."

She opened her mouth to offer to pay for it but closed

it before the words could escape. She wasn't sure Jace wouldn't take it in the same way he had her ill-thought-out suggestion he take the cash. She wasn't even sure why she'd said that, except that she hated thinking of how hard he'd been working to get out from under the mountain his worthless father had left for him.

And yet the fact that he was, that he had not simply run from it, was the very thing that filled her heart with such pride in him. No, running away was Cory's solution, not Jace's. Jace would never run from what he thought was right. It was one of the many reasons she loved him.

And there it was, in bold, glowing reality, the words formed in her mind formally for the first time.

She loved him. As an adult, not a naive child, she loved him.

"But she doesn't expect me back for it," Jace said. Then, with a pleased grin, "I thought this would take longer."

She wasn't certain what she'd just admitted to herself wasn't shining in her face, so she kept her head down as she said, "Then...you'll stay?"

"I'll stay," Jace said softly.

For a moment she still didn't dare look at him. And then, oddly, Cutter got down from his spot on the couch and walked to her. He plopped his chin on her knee, and she automatically reached to stroke his dark head. The moment her fingers touched the soft fur, calm seemed to flood her. And suddenly she didn't care if her feelings were written on her forehead in neon.

She looked at Jace.

He went very still. "Cassie," he whispered.

"Yes," she said.

And she meant it as answer to any and everything he might ask of her.

Chapter 19

Jace didn't think he'd ever in his life forget the way Cassie had looked at him that day at Foxworth. His entire future had seemed to unroll before him in her eyes. And for once that nagging voice in his head couldn't overpower it. Not the way he was feeling now.

He lay in bed—Cassie's bed—listening to the simple yet wonderful sounds of her drying her hair in the bathroom. With an effort he quashed the long-instilled feeling of guilt that he wasn't working. He couldn't quite believe they were really out from under.

He didn't have to quash thoughts of what would happen next, because he had put that out of his mind. He didn't want anything dampening this feeling, didn't want anything overshadowing these days and nights spent with her. They'd spent a lot of that time right here, in this bed, learning each other, and if either of them had thought the spark between them had been a fluke, they knew better now.

And since he'd had so little time for such things in his life, he was a bit amazed at how much he enjoyed even the simplest things, just talking with Cassie on a lazy morning, grinning when she laughed at his off-kilter jokes, even just shopping for a Thanksgiving dinner with her, since it helped him learn what she liked. And now that holiday was here, he was even looking forward to that despite wondering how it was going to feel to be face-to-face with Mrs. Alston, who had lived next door to them.

He was tempted to sneak into the bathroom now, see if he could lure Cassie back to bed just long enough to ease the urge that never seemed far away with her, but given the list she'd made of things to do today, he decided against it. Reluctantly. Besides, they were down to just a couple of condoms, and he wanted those for tonight.

They started on her list, Jace still feeling pretty blissful. He was a little concerned that his mother hadn't answered his phone call, but he thought she might have gone to work; she got paid double time for holidays at the clinic, and she was as much in the habit of always working as he was. And, he had to remember, out from under didn't mean ahead. But he shoved that aside, too, not wanting anything to shadow this time together.

He was amazed at, if nothing else, the array of dishes and utensils necessary to turn out a Grant-style Thanksgiving. He helped, although that mostly consisted of reaching, carrying and slicing various things at Cassie's direction. He didn't mind. He never would have thought doing kitchen tasks could be so…nice. Especially listening to Cassie hum happily as she worked.

When he finished with the carrots and handed them back to her, she'd smiled. "Funny…he's not even our dog, but I miss Cutter."

Jace just liked the way she said *our*. And told himself to savor it now, in case it all fell apart on him later, as things usually did.

"He's a pretty big personality," he agreed.

When the doorbell rang just after two, Cassie looked up from the turkey she'd been checking on, although Jace had decided it was coming out perfectly just from the luscious aroma. "A little early," she said as she closed the oven door again and headed for the front door. Jace followed, bracing himself for whichever guest it was.

But no amount of bracing could have prepared him for Cassie opening the door to his mother.

He stood there, feeling a little stunned, while Cassie exclaimed happily and threw her arms around the new arrival. When he embraced the woman who barely came up to his shoulder, all he could say was, "How?" in a bewildered voice.

"Those nice people who were helping you," she said, her eyes suspiciously wet. "They arranged it all, even that fancy car from the airport."

He saw the dark sedan pulling away from the curb and had the vague thought that he hoped the driver was getting that holiday double time.

"Foxworth?" Cassie said, and his mom nodded.

"They made it seem like I was doing them a favor," his mom said with a little laugh. The sound caught at Jace; she'd had so little reason to laugh for so long.

"I'm glad." Jace hugged her again.

"I missed you," she said simply. "And Mr. Crawford was so insistent, and very convincing on the phone."

"You should see him in person," Jace said.

Cassie laughed at that.

"I'd like to," his mother said.

"We invited him, and Cutter," Cassie said. "But…"

His mom nodded. "He's carrying some scars, that man. I could hear it just in his voice." Then she turned back to Cassie. "Ah, child, you look marvelous. It is so good to see you again."

"I am so glad you came," Cassie said, and her voice practically rang with emotion. "Jace was worried about you when you didn't answer his call."

Elizabeth turned, patted him on the shoulder. "He doesn't need to worry about me any longer. He needs to worry about himself now."

She looked from him to Cassie and back. And he thought he saw approval in her eyes. As if she'd guessed Cassie had become much more than his friend's sister to him.

"How long can you stay?" Cassie asked, still sounding delighted. "At least through the weekend, I hope?"

"Oh, you don't want another houseguest. I—"

"Of course we do!" Cassie insisted. "Let's get you settled in and then we can talk. We can—"

She stopped abruptly, and her gaze shot to his face. It took him a moment to realize what had hit her. The unoccupied guest room. She wasn't sure if he wanted his mother to know about them. Or…she wasn't sure if she herself wanted his mother to know. That thought rattled him a little. So he did the only thing he could think of and left it up to her.

"Your call," he said quietly.

"I'll get the guest room ready," Cassie said immediately. "While you and Jace…catch up."

When she was gone, his mother turned her gaze to him speculatively. He drew in a long breath, wondering where to start. And then she saved him the trouble.

"I always knew she adored you."

He let out that breath. "I don't know why, but she still does."

"That's obvious. I've waited a very long time to see a good woman look at my son like she just did."

"You ain't seen nothing yet," he said, and he couldn't stop the crooked grin that curved his mouth.

This tiny woman who had withstood so much, had worked so hard, put her arms around him in a fierce hug.

"And I've waited even longer to see you smile like that. It seems wrong to say, but your father walking out on us was the best thing that ever happened."

"Yes." Jace said it in simple agreement, for there was no doubt in his mind she was right.

"I should have walked out on him long before."

Jace drew back and looked down at her. "None of that. I've sworn off looking backward. We've learned what we needed to from it, now it's all forward."

"You've gotten very wise, my son," she said with a smile. Then for a moment she just looked at him. "She makes you very happy, doesn't she."

It wasn't really a question, but he answered anyway. "More than I thought possible."

"Then I'm delighted. For both of you."

Cassie would have left them to talk, but his mom insisted on helping in the kitchen. She and Cassie seemed to rub along well, and for a moment he just watched them, thinking as he watched Cassie laugh and his mother smile widely that he didn't think he could hold another ounce of that happiness.

"Oh," his mother said, stopping in the middle of setting plates on the table, "I forgot. I talked to my boss before I left. I'm getting a promotion to shift supervisor."

Jace stared, then grinned. "About time."

"And it's a nice raise," she added, with a look that told him once more that she would be all right.

When Mrs. Alston arrived on the dot of four, she took one look at his mother and enveloped her in a warm hug. And then, to his surprise, she did the same to Jace, murmuring, "It's so good to see you both, out from under that man and smiling." Jace was too happy to feel embarrassed; besides, he'd already guessed that living next door she'd heard a lot. But when she added, "I always thought you were stronger than he was, and now I see I was right," he shook his head and let out a small laugh. "Don't you deny it. It takes a lot of strength to take what he dished out and turn out a good, strong person."

"Amen." It was Cassie, pausing in her bustling to come up behind him and give him a hug.

"And you, m'girl, I see you finally got what you always wanted. And a handsome one he turned out to be!"

There was such a delighted twinkle in his former neighbor's eyes that both he and Cassie laughed.

When May arrived with her seven-year-old son, Mikhail, the boy seemed fascinated with Jace. Instinctively Jace crouched to shake the boy's solemnly offered hand.

"It's just you and me with all these ladies, so we gotta stick together, okay?"

Wide-eyed, Mikhail nodded, but a pleased smile crossed his face. And when he stood up and saw Cassie watching him, he thought her eyes looked a little damp. Another piece of that future rolled out in front of him. A child of theirs, one day? Did he have the nerve for that? The strength not to pass along what had been done to him?

He was still pondering that halfway through the meal, when everything had been tasted and pronounced delicious, and Mikhail had leaned over and whispered to him that his mom had brought her really good pie for after and he should save room.

When everyone had gone, Jace felt oddly tired. Socializing had been one of the first things to fall off the agenda in those tight days, and he wasn't used to it. A glance at his mother told him she was feeling the same, although she had more reason; traveling was tiring in itself. They sat and talked for a while, his mother making so clear she approved that Cassie was glowing, while he dared to hope the rough patch was really over, that it really was all forward now.

At nine his mother excused herself to go to bed, admitting the long day and wonderful meal had caught up with her. Cassie went with her to make sure she had all she needed, and watching the two of them only expanded the hope he was feeling.

He was also feeling a bit sleepy himself, so when the sound came from the front door it took him a moment to react. Maybe Mrs. Alston, or May—or Mikhail—had forgotten something. He even glanced around to see if the boy's handheld game was anywhere in sight. But then he realized whoever was at the door hadn't rung the bell or knocked.

They'd put a key in the lock.

He was on his feet in an instant. And at the door before it had swung more than a foot open. He stared.

"Hey, you're here!" the man on the porch said cheerfully. "Happy turkey day!"

Cory.

"She was really tired. She went out instantly. Turkey will do that to you," Cassidy was saying as she came back into the living room. And stopped in her tracks when she saw her brother standing just inside the front door. Jace was beside him, so tense she could feel it from here.

"Cory," she whispered, unable to come up with another word.

Her brother took two long strides toward her and swept her up in a bear hug. She didn't hug him back.

"Hey, little sis. You look great." Cory looked suddenly curious. "Really great."

She finally got her mouth working, and her words came out snappishly, since if she looked so much better than when he'd been here four months ago, it was because of how she'd been spending her time with Jace. "For a bookish little nerd?"

Cory looked her up and down. "I think you've left that behind."

She freed herself and took a half step back to look at him. It had always irritated her that he looked so much like their father but had so few of his sterling qualities. But he didn't look much like Dad now. In fact, he didn't even look much like himself, at least compared to the last time she'd seen him. He'd buzzed his hair, which had always been a bit long. Unlike Jace, that had been by choice, not because he couldn't afford a haircut. His eyes were the same, their father's warm brown, but even they seemed different because his gaze was so restless, darting around. And she wondered how much of her changed assessment of her brother stemmed from what she now knew of him.

He was also a little too slick, wearing a suit and dress shirt that looked new, although he'd forgone a tie. And she realized that she preferred Jace's worn jeans and T-shirts to this.

The moment she thought it, Jace was at her side. Just his presence calmed her. And reminded her.

"Spend a little of that cash on yourself, did you?" she asked, not bothering to rein in the sarcasm. But in that moment she was glad the guest room was at the far end of the house; Jace's mom wouldn't hear them.

Cory's eyes lit up. He looked at Jace. "I knew you'd figure it out and find it. You recognized the lever from that old well water line, didn't you?"

"Yeah," Jace said flatly.

"Let me rephrase what I said," Cassidy said coldly. "You spent a little of that *stolen* cash on yourself."

Surprise showed on Cory's face. "Um…stolen?"

"We know it all, Cory," Jace said. "Who you stole it from, when, and that you didn't have it on you when you got arrested in St. George."

The surprise turned to shock. Cory gaped at them both, apparently so stunned at their knowledge he couldn't even think of one of his usual snappy comebacks.

"When did you go from being just stupid to being a stupid thief?" Cassidy demanded.

"Hey, now," her brother protested. "That's harsh."

"Did you really think I'd just…take that money?"

"Why not? It's not like the guys I got it from are up-standing citizens."

"We found that out," Jace snapped, "when they came after Cassie."

Cory drew back. "What?"

He sounded so surprised, words burst from Cassidy. "Oh, for God's sake, Cory, what did you think would happen?"

"But I never told them about you!"

"Or where I lived?"

"Of course not. I mean, they knew the town I was from, but—"

"Is this address still on your driver's license?" She didn't feel at all guilty about peppering him with questions, not after watching Jace—and Cutter—take on a man with a gun because of what her idiot brother had done.

"Well, yeah, but they never saw that, either!"

"And the shop?" Jace asked. "You never mentioned that, either?"

"I…"

The truth was evident in the furtive way he avoided Jace's accusing gaze.

"So you mentioned the one flower shop in a town with

a population below three thousand, and you're surprised they were able to track her down?" Jace demanded.

"That was before," Cory protested. "I didn't know who they were then."

"And before you had the brilliant idea to steal from one of the nastiest gangs in the city?"

"I… It was right there, unguarded, and I had a way out…"

Cassidy groaned. "My God, Cory. Do you have any idea of the size of the mess you've gotten yourself—and me—into?"

"Well, that's thanks for you," Cory said, regaining a bit of his usual demeanor.

"Pardon me for not being thankful you left me stolen money and made me a target," she snapped.

"I never meant to—"

"You never do!" Cassidy tried to rein in her temper, not wanting to wake up Jace's mom.

Cory glanced at Jace, as if he thought he might find support there from his once best friend. Jace glared at him. "You know," he said, his tone dripping ice, "if doing the same thing over and over and expecting different results is insanity, then doing the same *stupid* thing over and over must just make you stupider."

"Oh, yeah?" was Cory's brilliant response. He looked Jace up and down. "I guess that's why you look like you got dressed out of a charity bin, because you're so smart?"

For the first time in her life, Cassidy wanted to slap someone. Hard. She'd never figured it would be her own brother. She even moved to do it, but Jace, as if he'd read her mind, put a hand on her arm to stop her.

"I'll take what I've got over looking like a two-bit hustler," Jace said coolly.

"Better than staying here, working in a stupid flower shop."

"That *stupid* shop fed you, clothed you and kept a roof over your head," Cassidy snapped, and at least Cory had the grace to look a bit guilty.

"You never did appreciate what you had," Jace said.

Cory's head came up sharply as he glared at his one-time best friend. "But you did, didn't you? You think I don't know they used to wish you were their son instead of me?"

Jace drew back as Cassidy gasped. "That's not true and you know it, Cory! They wished Jace was theirs, yes, because his life sucked, but it was not instead of you. They had enough love for all of us."

She glanced at Jace, who was staring at her as if he'd never realized until this moment exactly how strongly her parents had felt about him. But she went back to her brother and kept going.

"They worried about you. Stressed over you. Wondered what they'd done wrong. But most of all they loved you. So much. How can you be like this?"

Cory flushed. "Look, obviously I'm not welcome here. In my own house, by the way."

"Half," Cassidy snapped.

"Fine. I was going to crash here, but—"

"Sorry, the guest room's occupied."

Cory looked as if it were finally getting through to him just how angry she was. "Okay, okay. I just came by to get some of the cash, then I'll be out of your hair, dear sister."

"You mean you didn't just want to spend Thanksgiving with your beloved sister?" Cassidy said, sweetness fairly dripping from her words now.

"You want the cash, you'll have to go claim it from the cops," Jace said, sounding like he wished Cory would.

Her brother stared at them both. "You…you gave it to the cops?"

"Of course we did!" she snapped.

"I risked my life for that money!"

"And without thinking, as usual, you risked mine, and Jace's and Cutter's and—"

"Who the hell is Cutter?"

Leave it to her brother to fixate on that. "Never mind. If that's all you came here for, you can leave."

"Why are you so mad? I'm the one who should be ticked off. I can't believe you gave my money to the cops."

"I'd guess she's mad because you think it's your money," Jace said, drawing Cory's attention.

"Great. Never expected you to go all law and order on me. I was going to split it, after all. Three ways, me, you and my sister."

Cassidy hadn't thought she could be more disgusted. But she saw a chance to confirm something. "Why were you so sure Jace would be here?"

Cory looked puzzled then. "Because he promised."

"So you're not so far gone you don't see that," she said, reaching out to take Jace's hand.

"Jace always keeps his word," he said with a shrug, as if it meant nothing.

"As opposed to you. Where the hell did you get all this…flakiness? Why do you always have to look for the easy way?"

Cory's gaze flicked back to Jace. "Because I didn't want to live like him."

She felt Jace go still. Through his fingers she felt his sudden tension. Before he could say anything, she spoke softly. "While I want that more than anything."

"You'd like to be struggling?" Cory asked incredulously. "You saying you don't want to be rich?"

"Not if it means I have to go against everything I believe. I want," she said slowly, "to be happy, and to share that happiness with someone, to be like our parents, part of a unit that when it came down to it, always stood together."

Cory snorted. "Welcome to today's world, little sister. It doesn't work like that anymore."

"If you truly believe that, then I feel sorry for you. And Mom and Dad wouldn't even recognize you anymore."

"Oh, that's it, throw them in my face, like you always do."

"Cory?" Something in Jace's voice made her brother shift his gaze to him. "Shut the hell up."

He didn't say it loudly, not even angrily, but Cassidy thought only an utter fool would ignore him. But then again, it seemed Cory had become just that.

The landline phone rang, startling them all. Jace was closest and grabbed it, probably hoping it hadn't awakened his weary mother.

"Hello?" A split-second pause. "Yeah. What's—"

He went quiet. Too quiet. And a tension much greater

than when he'd been angry at Cory stole over him. She saw his knuckles whiten as his grip tightened around the phone receiver. And when he spoke again, his words were clearly answers to what he'd been asked, short, sharp, and furious.

"Flare. Possibly. No idea." Another pause as he listened. "All right. Yes. No matter what."

He set the phone down in the charger with far more care than necessary. Cassidy watched him, holding her breath. Even Cory seemed to realize something was up, because his brow was furrowed.

Jace turned around. His gaze zeroed in on her brother.

"You son of a bitch," Jace spat out. He put Cory on the floor with one swift, frighteningly solid punch to the jaw.

"Hey! What the hell was that for?" Cory scrabbled backward on the floor, looking ridiculously like the crabs they used to hunt for on trips to the beach. Her brother glanced at her, as if looking for support. She only waited for Jace to explain.

"You brought them with you," Jace snapped.

Chapter 20

Jace spun around to look at Cassie. His Cassie. Who was looking more than a little stunned.

"How…?" she asked.

"Rafe. Cutter. They're outside."

"They saw them?"

He understood that she'd hoped it was a mistake. So had he. For a moment his stomach knotted at the thought of the danger. And of his mother, who had already endured so much, asleep in the back room. Everyone he loved was here, in this house. And suddenly he understood the men in situations like these, for right now he knew he would defend them to the death.

He shoved the fear aside. There was no room or time for it.

"Both ends of the block. Two cars. We wouldn't make it to your car, or if we did they'd block us. Are all the doors and windows locked?"

"Yes. Except…" She glanced at the front door that Cory had unlocked. Quickly he stepped over and flipped the dead bolt.

"I saw that flare gun in his old room." He didn't even say Cory's name. "Does it work? Are there flares?"

"It's old, from when we had the boat, but... I don't know that it doesn't. And there's about a half box of flares. I saw them when we were clearing up."

"You messed with my room?" Cory bleated.

"That *shut the hell up* is still in effect," Jace said without even looking at him. "Any other weapons?"

"I don't—Dad used to have a rifle he used to take with us on the boat, just in case, but—"

"Permission to speak?" Cory said, managing to sound offended. "Dad's old plinking rifle is out in the shed. But it's only a .22."

"It's a weapon." Jace looked at Cory as he spoke, not bothering to hide his anger and disgust.

Cory looked back warily as he rubbed at his jaw. "They're really out there?"

"Don't waste time. Go get the rifle. Ammo if there is any." Cory looked doubtful. "Or run," Jace suggested coldly. "It's what you do best."

"I'll get it," Cassie said.

"No, I will," Cory said, although he sounded beyond reluctant. "I know where it is."

"I wouldn't turn on any lights," Jace suggested, and Cory's expression became even more frightened. But he headed for the kitchen and the back door—with the window Jace had boarded up—to the yard where the shed was.

"Think he'll come back?" Cassie asked, watching her brother go with a coolly assessing look that made Jace's stomach knot again. She shouldn't have to look like that, feel like that, not about her own brother. But he wouldn't lie to her.

"I don't know."

She didn't seem to dwell on it. He began to look around for anything else that might serve as a weapon. He figured they had minutes at most, and only that if the gang members outside were cautious.

"How did Rafe know?" Cassie asked, following him into the kitchen, where he took out the three biggest knives she had. "Why is he even around here?"

"Cutter, he said. And that he'd explain later." He smiled despite his trepidation when she added a small, heavy hammer with ominous-looking points on the head.

"Meat tenderizer," she explained, and his smile widened at the images that called up. Then, "They followed Cory here?"

"Best guess," Jace said, heading back into the much tidier room that had once been Cory's. He'd seen, maybe in the closet… There, an old, scuffed baseball bat. He added it to the collection on the counter.

Not much to go up against a bunch of big-city gangbangers.

The back door swung open. "It's me." Cory's voice came, a little tremulous. "They're out there. I saw movement down by a car in the alley. Behind Mrs. Alston's."

Since Jace hadn't had any doubts—if Rafe said they were here, they were here—he didn't respond to that. But when Cory set down the long zippered case and two boxes of bullets labeled ".22LR," he looked at the man who had once been his best friend.

"Do you know how to shoot that thing?"

"I know how," Cory said cautiously, "but…my sister was a better shot with it."

Jace frowned as he looked at Cassie. "I was," she protested.

"I wasn't doubting that for an instant," he said. "I just don't like the idea of you being the one to have to shoot."

"I can. And I will."

"I know," Jace said softly. And for just that instant it was all there between them, crackling and alive and utterly connected.

The landline rang again, and Jace spared a split second to wish they still had the much more subtle Foxworth cell phones.

Rafe didn't waste time. "I'm sending Cutter to you. He'll warn you when they're closing and show you where they are."

"Will he be safe?"

"He can move like a shadow when need be. I've seen eight, four in each car, but can't swear that's all." Eight. Jace swallowed. "Assume they're all armed, possibly multiple firearms per. Sheriff's on the way, but…"

"I know," Jace said, knowing that with the limited number of deputies to cover the whole county, it would probably take more time than they had. "We've got a .22 rifle that looks functional, a flare gun and a half dozen flares, then we're down to hand weapons."

"If they start your way, I'll take out as many as I can, but I can't guarantee one might not get through." Jace's eyes widened. One? Out of eight? Who the hell was Rafe Crawford, anyway? "Watch all sides, and up. Make sure the cameras are on. Don't shoot first unless they breach."

That abruptly, he was gone. As Jace replaced the receiver, there was a sound from the door Cory had come in. Scratching. Cory jumped; Cassie just looked at Jace. Then he heard a low whuff.

"Cutter," he said, and without a word Cassie turned to go let the dog in. He looked at the man who had once been his best friend, now apparently motionless with fear. "She's worth ten of you—you know that, don't you?"

Cory's eyes widened, then narrowed. "So that's it, huh?"

Jace ignored him, because Cassie was coming back, Cutter at her heels. There was nothing of the playful, sometimes silly companion in the animal now; he was all business, and it showed. The dog came over and briefly nudged his hand in acknowledgment, and Jace had to admit he felt ridiculously better with Cutter here.

"So," Cory said to his sister, his tone rather snarky, "I see you finally got what you always wanted."

Cassie stopped, staring at her brother. "In the middle of what you brought down on us, that's what you've got?"

Cutter gave a low, short growl, as if in warning, as he looked at the newcomer. Cory backed up a step. "Just trying to look out for my little sister," he said hastily.

"She's not yours to look out for anymore," Jace snapped at him. "She's mine."

He heard Cassie's quick intake of breath. Realized he'd never really said the words. He'd done his best to show her, but he'd been too much of a coward to say the words for fear she didn't feel the same, that he'd read her wrong, that once this was over and she didn't need him, she wouldn't want him anymore.

She was staring at him now, and for a moment he was terrified of what she might say. That she might not like what he'd said. That she really didn't feel—

"And you mine," she said softly, cutting off his thoughts and his breath.

"Cassie—"

"We'll work it all out later," she said.

And as he watched Cutter begin what appeared to be circuits of the house, as if he were listening in all directions, he realized the truth of her words—there was no time for this now.

"Now we just have to make sure there is a later," he said grimly.

And he would. Somehow, he would.

Jace figured he'd be able to tell how close they were by how Cutter reacted. If he just growled a warning, they were coming. If he broke into ferocious barking, they were close.

If he tried to claw his way through a wall, they were here.

He felt way out of his depth, but there was no time for that. The only advantage he could see was that those guys out there didn't know they knew they were coming. They didn't have the element of surprise, which they were likely counting on.

He walked to the kitchen counter, picked up the flare gun and loaded it, and stuck the rest of the flares in his pockets. Then he looked at Cassie, who was checking her cell phone to make sure the Foxworth cameras Rafe had not yet removed were rolling. He had a sudden vision of some crazy battle footage playing in a courtroom, and shoved it out of his mind; time enough to worry about that later. After they survived this.

"Dining room, I think," he said to her. "Center of the house, means they'd have to come through the rest of the place to get to us." She nodded, obviously scared but standing firm. "Can you use the rifle on a person if you have to?"

"If they break in? Yes."

Although he could hear she was scared, there was no hesitation in her voice. He nodded. "Rafe said don't shoot first unless they get in. Remember it'll likely take several rounds from a .22 to even slow somebody down." Cassie nodded. "And don't shoot at all, unless he—or they—get past me and Cutter."

Cassie shook her head then. "I'll stick to that, unless you're getting hurt. Then all bets are off. I'll stick it in his ear and shoot."

It was not a phrase that should fill him with happiness, but here and now it did. And Jace couldn't help grinning, because he knew she meant it.

"What am I supposed to do?" Cory asked.

"I think you've already done enough," Cassie snapped with a look at her brother Jace didn't ever want to see turned on him.

Cory winced and looked at least a little guilty. "Take your pick of what's left or go hide in a closet, I don't care," Jace said.

"Shouldn't we wake your mother?" Cassie asked,

turning back to him. "It might be better if we were all in the same room. I don't like her back there alone."

For a brief moment, he just looked at her. There was nothing but pure concern and love in her expression, and he could kiss her for it.

Hell with it, he thought, and did kiss her.

"Please," Cory griped. "Now?"

"Third and last time, shut up," Jace said.

Cassie gave her brother a look that said much the same. "I'll go get her. And try to explain. Only right, since it's my idiot brother who did this."

Cutter was making circuits of the house, pausing by doors and windows as if he had somehow already made note of the vulnerable points. Jace wondered if the dog truly realized what was happening. It certainly seemed like he did. Maybe he'd had some military training or something. He'd never asked Rafe about the dog's past.

He'd almost expected to hear gunshots. He remembered that lethal-looking rifle Rafe had carried. But there were none. As silent seconds ticked off, he tried to imagine what the Foxworth man was doing out there. He couldn't. He didn't have that kind of knowledge or experience. So he'd better focus on what he did know. Somewhat belatedly he thought of blockading the vulnerable points and snapped at Cory to help him move furniture. Chairs against doors, the sofa shoved against the heavy drapes at the front windows, the table in the kitchen against the back window so they'd have to clamber over it—anything that would slow them down even a second or two.

He'd just turned around as Cassie came into the

dining room with his mother, who looked surprisingly alert, considering. He didn't know what Cassie had told her, but she surveyed the remaining weapons and picked up the baseball bat.

"I used to be a fair softball player in my day," she said calmly.

Cassie glanced at Jace, smiling widely, and he grinned at them both. For some reason his mother's calm reaction calmed him as well. And Cassie, apparently, because she hugged his mom and then picked up the rifle. She'd loaded it earlier, but now she opened the remaining half-full box of bullets and stuck it in the back pocket of her jeans.

"Kind of old. Hope they don't blow up in the chamber," she said cheerfully. "Then I'll have to use it as a club."

In that moment, despite it all, Jace felt like the luckiest guy in the world to have these two women in his life.

He heard a loud pop from outside, but from a distance. Shot, or backfire? Another came, and his gut went with shot. He and Cassie exchanged a tense glance.

"Let the show begin," his mother said with the same determination he'd always heard from her. Cassie put an arm around her and squeezed. And when his mother looked up at the woman he loved with a wide smile, he again had the flash of a future brighter than he'd ever pictured before. And he dared to hope.

But first they had to survive tonight.

And then Cutter growled from the family room in back. Jace spun around and headed that way. Before he'd even gotten there, the growl erupted into that furious barking. It suddenly hit him that if it were him breaking in, the first thing he'd want to do was shut up the dog. And the easiest way to do that would be with a bullet.

"Cutter!"

He said it urgently, with no idea of whether the dog would even listen to him. The barking, to his surprise, ceased. "I've got it, quiet now," he urged. And to his even greater surprise, the dog came over to stand beside him. Quietly. As if he'd only needed to be sure Jace understood the threat was here.

He heard Cassie come in. Thought quickly. "Over there, by the light switch," he whispered. "That'll give you a better angle. If I yell 'now,' or they get past me, flip the light on."

She didn't question him, just went, and when she was there held the rifle ready, with one elbow close enough to flip up the switch.

They waited. Cutter stood with eyes, ears and nose focused on that back door. In the instant Jace thought he saw a shadow move outside, the dog shifted slightly, taking a couple of steps toward the window in the far corner of the room. The stationary one that, he remembered, didn't have a screen to remove. And was also at the darkest corner of the house.

Cutter looked back at him. "Got it, boy," he whispered and moved that direction.

The breaking of glass seemed loud in the silence. Jace waited, flare gun in his hand. Oddly, Cutter waited, too. He must have been trained—any ordinary dog probably would have charged the intruder by now.

There was the fainter tinkle of smaller pieces of glass falling. And then things seemed to shift, and a man-shaped shadow separated from the darkness outside and started to climb inside. The shadow of the first hand in seemed misshapen.

Because he's holding a gun.

Jace held his breath. Reached to touch Cutter with his free hand. If the dog charged now...but he held. He wanted this guy inside, so there could be no question.

And then he was. Jace fired the flare. It lit up the room in vivid red light in the instant before it hit the intruder. The man yelled, reeled back against the wall. He was slapping wildly at his side where the flare had ignited his clothing.

"Now!" he yelled.

Both Cassie and Cutter reacted instantly. The room light came on. The dog launched at the man. Jace reloaded the flare gun as he followed. Cutter had the man's gun arm by the wrist. He tried to shove the dog away with his other hand. Jace stomped on his gun arm, hard. And then Cassie was there. As promised, she jammed the barrel of the rifle practically into the man's ear. He froze. Then for good measure, his mother arrived and tapped the other side of his head with the bat.

He stared down at the man, distracted momentarily by his odd appearance—half his head shaved, the other sporting hair long enough to be braided with colored cords. Not, he thought, subtle.

Cutter whined, and after a look as if to make sure they had it under control, he trotted toward the back door, his tail wagging.

"Yo, the house!"

Rafe. Jace let out a breath he hadn't been aware of holding.

"Cory, do something useful and let him in," he said.

Apparently thoroughly chastened by the shock of what had just happened, Cory was silent as he went to the back door, pushed the chair Jace had shoved there out of the way and opened the door.

Rafe stepped inside, took a look at the scene before him, then lifted his head to look at the three of them. One corner of his mouth curled upward, and he nodded in approval.

"All over now but the paperwork," Rafe said.

"You got the rest of them?" Jace asked.

"They're in various stages of injury and confinement," the man said unconcernedly, as if taking down seven armed men was all in a day's work. And Jace had the feeling that, at least at one time, it had been for him.

"We heard shots," Cassie said, looking Rafe up and down in obvious concern.

"No hits," Rafe said.

Cutter gave a happy little woof, all right with his world again. It was over.

Chapter 21

"You'll be fine. The video makes it clear he broke in and was armed," Rafe said.

Cassidy nodded. The last thing she wanted right now was to deal with some kind of criminal charges for defending her own home.

"And your brother... Gavin will get him the best deal they'll give."

She nodded again, having no doubt that was true. The lawyer hadn't become a household name, still remembered years after he'd left his practice, by not being good at what he did. Sometime she would like to hear the story behind what had made him drop off the map like that.

But right now she was content with knowing he would work out a deal that just might keep her brother out of jail. Cory had reluctantly agreed to tell what he knew about the gang and their dealings with drugs and the protection racket, in return for leniency, maybe even immunity if it came down to him testifying at a trial.

"Now will you finally get some sleep?" she asked.

Rafe smiled at her. "Maybe." His gaze shifted to Jace. "My boss will want to talk with you when they get back."

Jace looked puzzled, but said, "Okay."

Cassidy figured it would be like a debriefing; the man with his name on the operation probably liked to keep track of what happened in his absence.

"We'll be sure and tell him you were a great front man," Cassidy teased.

Rafe drew back slightly. "Please don't," he said, rather fervently.

Jace chuckled. "Afraid he'll expect more of the same?"

"Something like that," Rafe said wryly. "He and Hayley are much, much better at it."

"And this guy?" Cassidy asked, reaching down to scratch Cutter's ears.

"He's the best of all," Rafe said. "I wouldn't have gotten here in time if not for thim. He was so restless I knew something was up. Then he started that barking. Took him outside, and he went straight for my car. And the minute I got in he started giving directions."

Cassidy stared at him, but she was smiling. "Directions?"

"Any time I would have made a wrong turn he started in again. Didn't take long to realize where we were headed."

She glanced at Jace, who was grinning.

And later, as they got in her car to leave Foxworth, likely for the last time, all Cassidy could think was that she was going to really miss both of them.

* * *

Jace sat in Cassie's living room looking at Quinn Foxworth, who was studying him so intently he felt more than a little edgy. If Rafe was intimidating, this man was…impressive. He'd arrived Sunday evening, just after they'd come back from taking his mom to the airport. Her departure wasn't sad, and Jace could still hear her final words to him.

You've taken care of me much longer than you should have had to. Now take care of yourself, and that girl you love.

"Rafe says you think differently," Quinn said.

"So I've been told," he answered, rather glumly.

"But you get to the right place."

"Most of the time." He wondered why it mattered to the head of Foxworth, now that it was all over. "But by way of tangents that don't…fit."

"Rafe also said you learn and adapt. Quickly."

Jace couldn't deny that pleased him. "I would never argue with Rafe Crawford," he said carefully.

Quinn laughed. "So, you're smart, too."

Jace studied the man across from him for a moment. "Is he always…so alone?"

Something flickered in Quinn's eyes. "It's his choice. Every one of us would have loved to have him with us for Thanksgiving. But he wouldn't, so we left Cutter to watch over him."

"A job he's exceptionally good at," Jace said, thinking he'd had firsthand experience with that.

"He is indeed." Quinn's tone changed—back to business. "Can you focus when you have to?"

Jace frowned. "Yes."

"Do you forget mundane things like paying the bills and keeping appointments?"

Jace shifted uncomfortably now—he really didn't understand why Quinn was asking all this, but neither could he look the man in the eye and refuse to respond. Not after what they'd done for him and Cassie. So he gave him an honest answer.

"I…don't forget, but sometimes I have to scramble when I've been deep into something else."

Quinn only nodded. "So that something else gets it all?"

"Yeah," Jace said, wondering yet again what all this is about.

"Your mother's still in Southern California?" Jace blinked, brow furrowed at the non sequitur. But he nodded.

"I… Yeah. She doesn't need me like she did, she's making it on her own now, but still…"

"It's been a long haul." Jace nodded. "Worth it?" Quinn asked.

Jace sat up straighter. "Absolutely."

Quinn smiled then, and nodded himself. "I have three more questions for you, then."

"Only three?"

"Yes. One, do you want Foxworth to find your father?" Jace's breath left him in a rush. "What?"

"Seems like he should be made to face what he did," Quinn said. "Maybe even pay back a little."

"But…they said since he waited until I was eighteen…"

"Yes. Desertion and child support wouldn't apply. Proof of his full intention, I'd say. But all that's officially. I'm talking about Foxworth, and we do things differently. Besides, you might want to make him face how wrong he was about you."

Jace almost smiled. Because the memory of Cassie snapping out his father's name whenever he backslid always made him smile.

Chuck! Do you think I'm stupid, Jace Cahill?

Of course not. You're the smartest person I know.

Then why do you think I'd fall in love with a worthless guy?

"It doesn't matter to me what he thinks anymore," he answered Quinn quietly, steadily. "And I don't want him anywhere near my life now."

"Good answer," Quinn said. "Second question. Cassidy says you were going to be an architect, but your father's profligacy destroyed that dream. Do you want to go for it now?"

He felt really uncomfortable now. "Not an option."

"Foxworth has a scholarship program."

"I'm a little old to be—"

"That's the nice thing about Foxworth. We make those decisions."

Jace stared at the man. "I don't… Why would you do that?"

"It's what we do. Help people no one else will. The ones who fight hard and do what's right no matter the cost. You're one of those, Jace."

"I…" He was still a little stunned and shook his head sharply. "I don't think so." His mouth twisted wryly. "School is worse than working. They tend not to care if you get to the right answer if you didn't do it their way."

Quinn smiled. "All right. That brings me to the last question. Do you want to take your out-of-the-box thinking somewhere it will be appreciated? Work where that kind of thinking is the norm, not the exception?"

"Is there such a—" He cut himself off as something occurred to him.

"Yes," Quinn said as if he'd completed the question. "There is. And it happens we have a new office in Orange County that isn't quite fully staffed yet."

Jace stared at him. "Are you…offering me a job?"

"I am."

"Doing…what you did for us?"

Quinn nodded. "Who could understand it better than someone who's been at the bottom end of helpless?" And then Quinn Foxworth mentioned a salary that stunned him, compared to what he'd been eking out.

Jace was dumbfounded. He'd expected to find even the one job that had said he might be able to come back gone, and now Quinn Foxworth was dropping the chance of a lifetime into his lap?

"I… Wow." He swallowed. Hard. "I don't… I mean, if I started to make that kind of money, my father'd probably drop back into my life."

"Then Foxworth will take care of him," Quinn said, with a hint of steel in his voice that made Jace realize he'd not only have a job, he'd never have to worry about that again.

And then it hit him. He was talking about Southern California. Close to his mother, but a long way from Cassie.

"Let's get the other party involved in here," Quinn said, as if he'd read Jace's thoughts. "Cutter?"

The dog, who had been quietly lying at Quinn's feet, got up quickly and trotted toward the hallway. Cassie was in Cory's old room, cleaning out the last of the stuff. She would put what seemed of any value in storage, she said, pay for one month, and after that it was up to her brother. Given the legal proceedings would likely take some time, Jace could easily foresee it all ending up auctioned off. The thought didn't bother him in the least.

Cutter came back with Cassie, who looked curious.

"I gather you wanted me?"

Oh, yeah. Forever.

And Jace suddenly realized that not even what seemed like an impossible dream job would be worth leaving her. Yet unless he took this chance, he had nothing to offer her.

Quinn explained the situation concisely, then left them alone, except for Cutter, to discuss it.

"That's perfect," she said quickly. "You'd be great at it, and close to your mom but not so close she feels you don't have faith that she'll be fine."

That was an angle he'd never thought of. But he was too struck by her apparent eagerness that he take this job over a thousand miles away to dwell on it.

"You think I should take it?"

"Don't you?" she asked, sounding startled that he would even consider not taking it. "I mean, I know there's some tidying up here to do, but then there's nothing here—"

"Fine," he said abruptly, trying to hide the effects of whatever it was that had ripped apart inside him. "I'll do it. And be out of your hair as soon as I can."

She frowned. "Jace—"

"I get it. It's over, problem solved, so everything can get back to the way it was."

Her frown deepened. "Nothing will ever be the way it was again."

She had that right. "I can pack in five minutes," he said, standing up. Cutter got to his feet as well. "Then you can have your life back."

Her expression cleared, became one of understanding. "Chuck," she said, sharply. His gaze snapped back to her then. "You think you're leaving, just like that?"

"You told me I should take the job."

"And you should." He kept looking at her as she spoke, didn't even glance at Cutter when he trotted out of the room and into the hallway. "It's an amazing opportunity, isn't it?"

"Yes."

And didn't it just figure, that the only chance he had, the best chance he would probably ever have, would take him far away from the main reason he wanted to take it?

"And they're going to pay you, right?"

His mouth tightened. "More than I ever expected to make in my life."

"All right, then."

He couldn't help it, the words broke from him. "So that's it?"

Before she could answer, an odd noise from his right drew his attention. Cutter was backing through the hallway opening into the living room. And he was pulling something with him. It wasn't until he rounded the end of the couch Cassie was sitting on that he saw what it was.

A suitcase.

Cassie burst out laughing. "Ah, my fine boy, you found just what I needed! How did you know it was stashed under the bed?"

Just what she needed?

He sank back into the chair he'd vacated, feeling gobsmacked. There was only one interpretation of her words he could think of, but he couldn't quite believe it. She wouldn't, couldn't…could she? Not for him, not—
Chuck!

As if she'd said it again, it echoed in his head, that warning that he was letting that old, foul voice win.

Rebellion boiled up in him. He was not going to let that sperm donor take away the best thing that had ever happened to him. He looked at Cassie, who sat silently, waiting. Waiting for him to work his way through it, to beat back that evil voice.

"The shop," he began.

"May can run it as well as I can. That will give us time to decide whether to sell it, or maybe start a chain," she said, grinning at him.

"This place," he said, gesturing around them at the house.

"It's a place," she said. "It has meaning, but that meaning is in my heart more than in this building. And my heart's going with you, Jace, no matter where I am."

His own heart was hammering in his chest. When he thought he could do it steadily, he held her gaze and asked, "Will you come with me?"

The smile that lit her face then was, he knew, at far more than just the question. "Of course I will. You just try and go without me, Jace Cahill."

"I don't want to go anywhere without you."

"I want that fifty years," she said, holding his gaze.

He swallowed. Wondered if he could risk it. Then looked into her eyes and realized it wasn't a risk at all. "Oh, yeah? Well, I want that sixty," he said, meaning it more than he'd ever meant anything.

"Then we're agreed. But," she added wryly, "can we not tell my brother where we are?"

He laughed but then took in a long breath. "I'll always be grateful to him. He let me into his life, otherwise I'd have never known what it could be like. And I'd never have known you."

"Then maybe I'll speak to him again. Eventually."

He knew she would; Cassie loved completely. But the thought of her sibling made him think of something else, something he'd thought long decided for himself.

"Cassie, I… Kids. You'll want them, and you'd be so good at it, but I—"

"You'd never, ever pass it on, Jace, if that's what you're worried about. But if you can't get past that, we'll get a dog until you can." She grinned. "Maybe one like Cutter. That'd be like having a kid."

He couldn't help grinning back at her.

"Now," she said briskly, "shall we call your mom and tell her we're coming, or surprise her?"

It was very like Cassie to jump right into the logistics, but it moved him more than he could say that her first thought was of his mother.

"Surprise her, I think," he said after a moment. "She hasn't had enough good ones in her life."

"We'll just have to make sure that's all she gets from now on," she said.

"I love you, Cassie."

The words came without thought, without hesitation, from that place deep inside him that only she had ever reached.

"And I love you, as I always have," she said, her eyes so warm and her touch as she reached up to cup his cheek so soft he thought he was going burst with loving her. "Now why don't you go tell Mr. Foxworth that you accept, and then come help me pack. In the bedroom."

She added the last with that glint in her eye he'd come to know. Joyously. And the kind of certainty he'd never known welled up inside him until there was room for nothing else. Especially that voice.

So long, Chuck.

He turned to go find Quinn Foxworth.

* * * * *

COMING SOON!

We really hope you enjoyed reading this book. If you're looking for more romance, be sure to head to the shops when new books are available on

Thursday 4th April

To see which titles are coming soon, please visit

millsandboon.co.uk/nextmonth

LET'S TALK
Romance

For exclusive extracts, competitions
and special offers, find us online: